A Tale of the King

Arlene Bergen

Copyright © 2018 Arlene Bergen

All rights reserved.

ISBN:1975689046
ISBN-13: 9781975689049

DEDICATION

*For my darling children:
Shaymus, Koby, Max, and Skye
May your lives bring glory to the King*

CONTENTS:

Acknowledgements

Part One: The Garden

Chapters 1-11

Part Two: The Land of Nachash

Chapters 12-33

Part Three: All Things New

Chapters 34-38

ACKNOWLEDGMENTS

Rob, for all the times you smiled when I thought the story was great, and the times you encouraged me when I was sure it wasn't—even if those times were only ten minutes apart—thank you. We have dreamed side by side for over half our lives; there is no one I would rather dream with. I love you.

Thank you Shaymus, Koby, Max, and Skye, for your interest, encouragement, and support. You are my inspiration.

Dawne, thank you seems so small when I consider all the hours and effort you poured into editing. But thank you! Thank you for your keen eye, sharp mind, and soft heart. This is a better story because of you, and I am grateful!

PROLOGUE

The Duke's robes swirled around his feet as he strode through the palace hallway. His arrogance paid no mind to those scurrying aside to clear a path. He pushed past the first set of guards before slamming into a rock wall—Michael's chest.

"Step aside, Michael!" spat the Duke.

"Tread carefully, Nachash! You enter the presence of the King," warned Michael, unsheathing his sword.

The Duke defiantly brushed Michael's sword away before marching into the chamber. He lowered himself into a deeply exaggerated bow at the foot of the throne, then straightened to address the King.

"There is a matter of great importance we must discuss, O King," he demanded.

The King raised his eyebrows but didn't look surprised. "What is your concern, Nachash?"

"Your people are my concern," he asserted. "I've worked hard to earn my place in the Kingdom. I've proved competent at my position. There are many who serve under me, and yet, you demean me!"

"Nachash, we both know you have a position of authority among the palace staff. How have I demeaned you?" questioned the King.

"You say I have authority," Nachash gestured aggressively as he spoke, "but when I try to enter the garden and speak with the people, I'm denied entrance!"

The King's jaw tightened ominously. "The time hasn't been right."

Michael had followed Nachash into the chamber. Seeing the Duke's anger mount, he took a step closer to the throne to remind Nachash of the threat of his presence.

Michael shook his head. He could have guessed Nachash's issue would be with the people. Palace staff were forbidden from entering the gardens. They were kept separate from the people. Nachash, however, was obsessed with them.

Truthfully, the people were a subject of curiosity among all the palace staff. They knew the King delighted in them and that he entered the gardens daily to be with them. And they knew the King had a grand plan that involved the people. When the King discussed this plan privately with the Prince in the upper chambers, some overheard small snatches of it, but no one knew enough of the details to understand it.

Most of the palace staff accepted that this was the way the King had decided it would be. They trusted the King and believed he would tell them more when the time was right.

Not Nachash. He resented anything the King withheld from him.

Mindless to the mounting tension, Nachash pressed on. "We all know the possessive hold you have on these people, 'the apple of your eye,' you say. We know you selfishly keep them from us." The Duke stepped closer to the throne and motioned dangerously near the King's face. "But we've yet to meet one of them!"

"Remember your place, Nachash," warned the King.

"My place?" ground out Nachash. "What is my place, O King?"

"You serve me, as do the others," answered the King.

"I tire of serving you!" shouted Nachash. "We live as

servants in your Kingdom, waiting on you while you keep the best for yourself." Contempt twisted his features. "Is your ego so fragile, O King, that you're afraid of the consequences if you allow us access to your people?"

The King turned his head to gaze out the window. It framed a dense forest, beyond which lay the gardens. It was a long moment before the King answered.

"You don't understand the people, Nachash. I created them with a yearning, a need to adore. They serve because they're created to. It's their source of delight. But I've also given them a free will about whom they serve. It's part of my plan."

"Your plan," Nachash sneered scornfully. "Serve we must—with that I agree. It is *who* we serve that I question."

The King turned his piercing eyes toward the Duke. "Why are you really here, Nachash?"

The Duke's eyes glittered triumphantly. "Many of your servants have noticed my great strength. They admire my unrivalled beauty. I'm known for my intelligence and skill in commanding legions, and those who serve under me, adore me. They speak of making me king."

"You challenge me?"

"Yes, I challenge you!" roared Nachash. "I will be king! It is me they will serve!" Greedy anticipation dribbled down his chin in beads of spittle. "Your people will be mine!"

A collective gasp sounded throughout the chamber. Michael leapt between Nachash and the King, sword raised. Royal attendants who had trickled in during the exchange shifted nervously. Midnight-robed minions of Nachash crept from the shadows to the centre of the chamber.

Michael eyed their growing number warily and spoke loudly, "King, our greatest joy and desire is to serve you. Give the word and I'll remove Nachash." Michael expected his declaration of devotion to be echoed by cries of allegiance rather than nervous silence.

The King rose to his feet. With a gentle hand and easy pressure, he moved Michael aside and straightened to his full height, towering over Nachash. His voice shook the palace floor. "Servants of the palace, enter my chamber."

Royal attendants from all stations filed into the throne room, but the King's eyes never left the Duke's. When the chamber was full, the King gave his order. "Make your choice! Show your allegiance today and stand behind the one you wish to serve!"

Courtiers slid into place behind the Duke, whose chest swelled with pride.

It is odd how time can seem to race while at the same time standing still, Michael thought, as he watched it unfold. He saw Nachash exchange meaningful looks with his legion. The Duke lunged towards the King with a confidence spawned from intent older than the moment, and though Michael understood what was happening, he stood encapsulated in a single unit of time, unable to respond.

Suddenly, a powerful cry rang out, freeing his frozen limbs. Michael threw himself in front of the King to protect him from Nachash, but the King didn't need his protection. The Duke already lay on the floor at the King's feet, conscious, but completely unable to move. It seemed he'd been paralyzed by the same sound that had released Michael.

With the intense awareness that carried him through battle, Michael experienced the events in slow-motion. One by one, courtiers fell to their knees throughout the throne room as the cry grew in power. Michael turned his head to follow the source of the cry and saw it came from the King.

Quickly overcome by the commanding sound, Michael fell to the floor. His sword clattered across the marble as he pressed his hands over his ears to protect them from the dreadful roar.

As the King's cry resonated throughout the chamber, the distant beating of a pair of wings joined in, carrying it to a crescendo.

Michael's heart pounded in rhythm as these wings swept over the garden. He trembled like a young tree as they brushed low over the forest. His stomach felt caught up in their whirlwind as they rushed through the open window.

Michael shielded his eyes and watched a great eagle fly to hover above the King. He quaked when the eagle echoed back the King's cry.

Finally, the King held up his hand for silence. But rather than relief, the stillness that followed was like a thick and terrible presence. The King spoke into the silence with authority. Some resented it. Some submitted to it. No one questioned it.

"We will battle, Nachash," declared the King. "Not here. Not today. But fight we will. The war will be long and bloody, and you will win some of the battles. Yet know this: the outcome is sure. From this day forward, I'll allow you access to my people, but only because it has always been my plan. Starting today, the only service I'll receive will be from those who desire to give it."

When he finished speaking, the King raised his great finger and pointed to the men laying scattered around Nachash. He motioned to the door and bellowed, "Leave! Never again will you enter my palace! Get out!"

The Duke crawled from the King's presence, the bile of shame burning his throat. Safely outside the palace he vomited it out. "We will not stop! Not until every one of his prized people has been turned to our side! We will do whatever it takes to win their allegiance. He may be the all-powerful King, but I have the power to bring him great pain.

He can have the war, but this will be my victory: with every person I win over, I'll plunge the sword of suffering into his heart!"

****

Michael hurried to follow the King upstairs to the Prince's chambers, but the King slipped inside and shut the door firmly before Michael could catch up, leaving him outside.

Michael paced anxiously on his side of the closed door, desperate to know what was happening in that room. Life in the Kingdom had been turned on its head. He needed information to know what to do. Michael stopped pacing and pressed against the door. He stilled his breathing, trying to grab hold of the words the King was speaking to the Prince. Muffled voices pushed through the cracks in the wood as the King spoke.

"It's time. The plan has begun."

Unable to restrain himself, Michael threw his shoulder into the door and burst it open. Overcome with ardent devotion, he implored, "Give me the order, King! I can get rid of Nachash and his followers forever!"

At Michael's interruption, the King moved from the Prince's side and walked across the room to a wall of soaring windows. He shook his head. "That is not how it is to be."

Standing in front of the windows, the King looked

across the forest and into the gardens. He turned back to look at the Prince and a groan ripped from his chest. The King dropped into a nearby chair and cradled his head.

"My people," he moaned. Keening lament tore at Michael's heart as the King cried louder. "My son! My beloved son!"

Michael watched helplessly as the Prince knelt beside the King, and they wept.

Part One: The Garden

CHAPTER 1

Abigail hummed as she twirled to the strains of a melody dancing around in her head. It teased her, swirling just out of reach, tantalizing her to chase it, catch it, and transform it into a coherent song. Morning music practice was over so she skipped to the meadow, planning to pass time until the afternoon performance by day-dreaming in the sunshine.

Practise brought discipline, leisure spawned creativity, but performance birthed delight. Afternoon performances for the King were the high point of every day and, though the pattern was predictable, the thrill was new every morning. The people never tired of delighting their King.

Golden curls splayed around Abigail's head as she lay

on the bed of grass. The mid-day sun embraced her gently and she lifted her face to soak in its warmth. No sooner had she closed her eyes to dream, than a boisterous jostling caught her attention. A trio of warriors approached, humorously re-enacting their early morning maneuvers. Abigail sat up to watch. Seth happily shouted orders while Drew showed off his strength with focus and determination. Marc gleefully wove between the two, attempting to distract them.

Content to surrender her solitary dreams to their unbridled enthusiasm, Abigail waved at them. "Over here, come and join me!" she called. They smiled at her greeting and ambled towards her, flopping down in the harmony that characterized their friendship.

"During our drills this morning, we practised the formation that I created," boasted Seth.

Drew was quick to respond, "Tomorrow we're working on my ideas. They'll be even better!"

Abigail glanced over at Marc, sprawled out on the grass. "What about you, Marc? When do you get to show the warriors your battle technique?"

Marc shrugged lazily. "As long as I can drill with my friends and it's fast and exciting, it doesn't matter to me." He rolled onto his side to grin at Abigail. "Unless you're coming to watch. Then I'll pull out all the stops." Marc's deep brown eyes winked at her teasingly.

Abigail waved off his banter with a grin and a nod. "You enjoy drilling like I love my singing."

The three nodded enthusiastically. "It's what we were made to do, and the King loves to watch us," Seth replied. "Just like he loves to listen to you sing."

Abigail agreed. She couldn't explain her love for music and song; it was simply how she was made. And because it was her heart's greatest delight, she offered it to the King.

They chatted for a while before allowing quiet to settle over them. Lulled by the peace, Abigail allowed her thoughts to drift. Random meanderings soon followed a familiar trail and she closed her eyes and released her mind to take the journey through her favourite memory.

It always began with the weight of darkness, the heavy scent of the soil, and the void of silence. Then, in the buoyancy of light, the fragrance of fresh flowers, and the elusive strains of an ethereal melody, there was a startling change. Royal breath fused the dark with the light, the dirt with the flowers, and the silence with the music. Opened eyes saw the face of the King. Then her heart, which ached from a dichotomous pull between the common and the majestic, was soothed by the gentle love in his eyes.

The remembered moment was so vivid, Abigail

gasped softly and her eyes popped open. She saw Seth watching her.

"You're remembering the moment you woke up again, aren't you?" he asked.

Wanting to protect the intimacy of her thoughts, she turned her head from Seth, but still she questioned softly, "What was it like for you? Do you remember the moment you awoke?"

Seth was silent a moment before answering, "I don't think I'll ever forget it. I don't think we are meant to."

"What was the awakening like for you?" Abigail had heard his story before. Many times. But the people never grew tired of the awakening stories.

"For me it started with stillness. After the stillness came thunder. It was the sound of strength and power. Sometimes when I sit by the waterfall, I hear echoes of that first sound," Seth remembered.

"When I sit by the brook, and hear it gurgling over the rocks," Abigail whispered, "I can almost capture the music I first heard. The moment of awareness, the meeting of silence and sound, void and wholeness. And always his face, always the love."

Seth and Abigail turned to each other and spoke together, "And then there was the gasp."

Abigail nodded vigorously, eyes sparkling as Seth

continued. "At the very moment my eyes opened and he saw me look at him, I remember his sharp intake of breath. Our eyes met and his filled with delight. I saw him savour the satisfaction and joy of creation." Seth shook his head, contemplating the miracle of it all—a King in love with his creation.

Drew was never as quick to speak as Seth, but he was always listening. He'd followed their conversation and now sat up and crossed his arms over bent knees before joining in. "That's why we perform our hearts' delights for him, you know. We do it because of the joy it brings him and because we're compelled to. It's how we were made."

Three sets of eyes turned to Marc, leaving space for him to enter the conversation if he wanted to. Instead, he gave Drew a jesting shove before jumping up from the grass. "Sit here and reflect all you want. I'm off to find the King." Marc sauntered towards the central park where the King would be waiting. The great eagle already soared over the meeting place in invitation.

Abigail rose to follow her friends and soon merged in with the throngs of people moving towards the meeting place. Warriors, singers, gardeners, and wise ones all mingled together, eagerly chattering about their upcoming performance. Theodore's voice rose above the joyful babble as he came to walk beside her. "Good afternoon, Abigail! Do the singers have something new for the King today?"

"Well, we've been practising the Creation Song, but can only remember bits of it. Parts of the melody are clear for brief seconds, but then it fades out. We just can't quite grab hold of it, and the harmony has always been elusive. So today we'll sing the Song of the Garden. The King always seems to enjoy that one." Abigail smiled up at Theodore. He was one of the most respected wise ones, and she always enjoyed their conversations. "What about the wise ones? What will you be reading for the King today?"

Theodore slowed his walking and rubbed his chin. "Today we'll read one of my poems about the character of the King. It's a reflection on who he is and a reminder of his great love for us. We'll celebrate the magnificence of our environment and declare how its beauty reveals the King's care for us."

The longer he spoke the more animated his expression became. He stopped walking and thrust his finger upward to drive his point home, nearly shouting. "We culminate by celebrating our own creation. We, the pinnacle of his work, created for . . . for what?! Delight? Joy? Glory? His, not ours, mind you . . ." Theodore's voice trailed off, and Abigail could tell he was getting caught up in a tangle of thoughts.

She tugged on his sleeve. "Theodore, if we don't keep

walking, we'll be late for the King's visit." She feared he'd stay knotted up in thought on the side of the road for hours if she didn't urge him onward.

Theodore looked around with a start. "Right you are, my friend, right you are," he murmured, hurrying forward. "We mustn't be late for the King." His eyes lit up as he spotted the eagle circling above them.

Running off to join the singers, Abigail called back, laughing, "I look forward to your reading, Theodore."

Today's order of performance began with the warriors, continued with the reading of the wise men, and finished with the singers. Abigail heard the King exclaim on the magnificence of the flowers to the gardeners as she watched the warriors assemble in formation. When she stole a look at the gardeners she saw that they blushed under the King's approval.

Seth stood in front of the warriors, waiting for the King's signal to begin. It was obvious that he was eager to show his work to the King. A nod from the King brought a shouted command from Seth. The warriors leapt into action. They marched in opposing lines, meeting to parry, duck, tumble and re-form in perfect synchronization. They ended with a flourish and Abigail clapped enthusiastically, happy for her friend as he proudly accepted the accolades of the King.

The enthusiastic crowd always took time to settle down between performances. Young ones scrambled to find spots on or near the King's lap. Older ones stretched and shifted into comfortable positions while the wise ones prepared in the shade of the trees. When all were settled quietly, Theodore began to speak. His voice was deep and clear and spoke passionately of the King. It urged the people to bask in his love for them and to delight in his presence among them. The King beamed his approval at Theodore's words. Sometimes he nodded and bent low to whisper to the young ones on his lap.

The people had no real sense of time, only a sense of being. This was all they knew. The presence of the King soothed them. In his presence, peace and love surrounded them.

Theodore's speech wound to a close so Abigail moved to stand with the singers. When they received the signal to start, they lifted their voices, softly at first. The volume increased and Abigail's heart soared with the music. Nature seemed to join the crescendo; birds beat the rhythm with their wings, the brook bubbled a gentle harmony, rustling trees swayed and danced, joining the symphony. Creation celebrated under the gentle gaze of its creator.

The final strains of music faded and the King led a thunderous applause. "Exceptional, my singers! Absolutely brilliant! I have never enjoyed it more!" His powerful voice resonated with approval and it felt to Abigail like the first time she'd sung for him.

The day's performances came to a close but the people lingered, enjoying each other's company and the presence of the King.

*****

Nachash and his legions watched the King and his people from the shadows of the forest. "At last, we see his precious people," the Duke hissed to his followers.

"They hang onto his every word. He has their undivided attention," breathed one of the followers directly behind the Duke. "This is going to be harder than we thought."

The Duke snorted. "How wrong you are," he mocked. "They grovel, desiring to serve, wanting to please. We need only confuse their minds about who they serve."

"You might be beautiful, but there's no comparison between you and the King," Nachash's follower muttered. "I don't see how you'll achieve a switch in allegiance."

Nachash laughed cruelly. "Cunning and patience, my friend. We start slowly. First we plant the seed of doubt. We water the doubt until it takes root and grows." Nachash gained momentum as he continued. "Like a brook that becomes a raging river, we present them with options that seem innocent enough at first. After they've taken the first step, the second step will be easier. The time in between the second and third steps will be shorter, and the reward for our patience and persistence will be like a waterfall; they'll eventually be swept away by their choices, unable to turn back."

The Duke's followers gazed at him in awe. "But where do we start?"

Nachash smiled. "At the centre. We take the King out of the centre of their lives."

The outspoken follower shook his head in doubt. "I don't think it'll be that easy to replace the King with you."

Nachash grinned. "You're right. We won't replace the King with me. They'll be convinced much more quickly if it's not the King at the centre, and not the Duke at the centre, but themselves! We'll trick them into thinking they serve themselves and that their only allegiance is to themselves. Soon enough they'll know that in choosing to serve themselves, they've chosen to serve me."

The Duke's followers shook their heads, in awe of his cunning.

They glanced between the Duke and the people as the Duke's laugh drifted through the leafy trees.

*****

Abigail watched the King walk into the forest on his

way back to the palace. Immediately she knew a longing for tomorrow. Just before the King disappeared into the trees, she saw him stop and glance back. She followed his gaze to a distant grove of trees on the opposite side of the park. His expression changed. The King looked as if he were in pain. He clutched at his heart. Abigail tore her gaze from the King and looked at the grouping of trees that held his attention. She started in alarm. Unusual shapes distorted the shadows and the trunks seemed to move.

Abigail didn't know that it was fear that made her run to cover the distance between her, Theodore, and her warrior friends. Walking back from the gardens alone had never bothered her before. Today she couldn't ward off the chill that raced across her skin. Breathless, she caught up to the group and grabbed onto Seth's arm as unfamiliar feelings overtook her.

Seth glanced down at her in surprise. "Abigail, you look like something's wrong!" he exclaimed.

Abigail glanced back at the trees apprehensively, before laughing nervously, trying to shrug off her behaviour. "It's nothing. I just thought I saw something unusual in the forest."

Seth turned to study the treeline in concern. Shadows shifted in patterns inconsistent with the path of light. Disquiet nipped at his heels as he resumed walking, more quickly this time. Deep inside, he felt stirred to battle and didn't understand. This was a very different feeling than the one that drove him to practise and drill. This feeling was driven by a sense of urgency.

Theodore watched Seth walk quickly while throwing worried glances over his shoulder. He noted how Abigail clung to Seth's arm, pressing in as if she were cold despite the warmth of the garden. Narrowing his eyes, Theodore murmured anxiously, "There is something afoot!"

CHAPTER 2

Theodore suffered a restless night of sleep before waking early to pour over his scrolls. He combed through their words, looking for the inspiration he needed to write. Words wouldn't come. Ideas taunted him, scampering around the recesses of his brain, but they refused to emerge in any orderly fashion. Something niggled at him, wanting to be expressed, but he couldn't find any corresponding words to give it voice.

"Well," he finally exclaimed out loud, "there is but one thing to do. I'll go see the King!"

Theodore walked through the park, taking time to chat with the gardeners and admire their work. He waved at the singers practising under a canopy of branches, and saluted Drew as he led the warriors in their morning drills. He made his way to the edge of the brook, enjoying the gentle sound of the water, knowing the King would already be there. Theodore had never summoned the King. No one ever had. But they all knew that if they had need of him, he'd be there. It was as if the summons to meet came from the King himself.

The King smiled as Theodore approached. "Good morning, Theodore," greeted the King. "A lovely day for a stroll, wouldn't you say?"

Theodore laughed as he responded. "Good morning, my King! It is a perfect day filled with beauty, like every other." They ambled along the edge of the brook, enjoying each other's company before Theodore broke the comfortable silence. "My King, in my time of writing this morning there were thoughts in my head that I didn't understand. I can't express them, but I feel like I must because they will not leave."

The King led Theodore to a couple of smooth rocks where they sat down facing each other. He didn't respond but sat, gazing at Theodore, waiting. So Theodore continued speaking. "It's strange, but I feel that I must write, like it is my duty to, but I'm not sure what to write. It's why I sought you out this morning."

The King smiled at Theodore's words and patted his arm. "You bring me such delight, Theodore!"

Theodore nodded, pleased at the King's comment. "Each day in your Kingdom is a delight! We have the thrill of discovery and newness every morning. I am a man of many years, yet not a day has passed that I don't discover something fresh and exciting tucked away in some corner of the garden. You have designed a masterpiece that we will never tire of."

The King's smile faded as he murmured, "If only that were true."

Theodore frowned slightly at the King's words. "Whatever can you mean, King? How could we not delight in all that you have made for us?"

"Each day is new, Theodore," answered the King. "Take it for what it brings."

"There's change in the air. I sense it, but I don't understand it," insisted Theodore.

"I've put the ability to sense the unseen in some of you," responded the King. "You were right to bring what you don't understand to me." The King shifted slightly, looking closely into Theodore's eyes. His gaze penetrated as he spoke. "Write, Theodore. Write of the Prince. Write of the plan. Theodore, it has begun."

"You've spoken of the Prince before, and we look forward to meeting him," Theodore gushed. "Will it be soon?"

"You will meet him when the time is right," answered

the King. "It is all part of the plan."

"What is this plan, exactly?" questioned Theodore. "I feel like it would be helpful to have more details about it if I am supposed to write of it."

The King leaned forward intently, "Write, Theodore."

Theodore pulled out a scroll that he kept tucked in his belt and began to scribble as the King spoke.

"The plan is beautiful, but it will not look beautiful at times. It will unfold as it must, over its due course of time, but it will seem to you that it is taking longer than it should. The plan has seasons that will be painful and hard to understand."

Theodore furrowed his brow as he scrawled quickly across the scroll. "I don't understand, my King. You're using words I don't know. Time. Pain. Seasons. What are these?"

The King grasped Theodore's hands and stopped his writing. "You won't fully understand. Not while it's happening. You won't understand until the whole plan is complete. Can you trust me?"

Theodore wrenched his hands from the King's in shock. "How can you ask that? You're my King! Trusting you is all I know! It is all I've ever done!"

The King rose. He began to walk towards the forest and Theodore knew their time was coming to an end. "Write what I've told you, even if you don't see the sense in it. At the right time, you'll look back on what you've written and remember."

The eagle swirled above the King as he returned to the palace. "You're one of the wise ones. It's your duty to remind the people of what you know to be true. It's who I've created you to be." The King smiled back at Theodore. "You've done well, Theodore."

Theodore watched the King slip through the trees of the forest before hurrying back to his writing table. He was eager to record what had transpired between them. His thoughts were a bit of a jumble, but write he would, even if he didn't understand.

Why did the King speak of the unseen? Why did he question Theodore's trust? It made no sense! Yet, there was an urgency to his task today, pushing him to record each word that was spoken and to list the questions that remained.

CHAPTER 3

Abigail was leaving singing practice as Theodore rushed past her. She raised her hand to wave but he didn't even look up. "There's Theodore, lost deep in thought again," she surmised. There was no offence among the people so, rather than let her thoughts linger on Theodore's busyness, she directed them elsewhere.

Several days before, she'd been out walking and had come upon a hill she'd never seen before. Today she was eager to go exploring. Abigail hummed as she skipped through the gardens. The hill sat near the edge of the gardens and looked over the forest towards the palace rise on an opposite hill. Abigail reached the hill and climbed quickly, anticipating the view from the top. She crested the hill and wasn't disappointed.

The vision was glorious. The gardens spread beneath her, a patchwork quilt of jeweled tones and velvet textures enclosed within the towering walls of the Kingdom. The forest blanketed the valley between the hills, separating the garden and the palace mountain.

The palace rose from the pinnacle of the majestic mountain, sprawled across the westernmost edge of the horizon. It shimmered resplendent, transcending anything Abigail could have envisioned. Misty clouds hung suspended in the air, enveloping the palace in a veil that obscured a measure of its brilliance. Abigail rubbed her eyes, thankful for the covering of clouds, certain the palace would have blinded her had the clouds not been there.

"It is more beautiful than anything you've ever imagined, isn't it?" spoke a deep voice behind her.

Abigail whirled around at the interruption; she hadn't heard anyone approach. A man stood behind her, gazing at the palace. He was shockingly handsome, and Abigail couldn't help but stare in fascination. When he turned his penetrating gaze from the palace to her, Abigail quickly looked away from its intensity. Flustered by his attention, she pretended to be captivated by the view and murmured her agreement about the palace.

"It is far more wondrous on the inside."

Abigail jerked her head back to the man, surprised at his words. "No one has ever been inside the palace!" she exclaimed.

Though he shocked her, his allure was magnetic, and she couldn't resist the opportunity to scrutinize him. She knew he wasn't one of the people, but who else could he be? Unable to reign in her curiosity, Abigail questioned him. "I can see you're not one of the people, and now you say you have been inside the palace! Who are you?"

He flashed her a dazzling smile. "I'm a Duke. My name is Nachash."

Abigail's mouth dropped open. "You're one of the King's servants, from inside the palace?" she gasped.

"I am," he stated proudly. "Second only to the King."

"We—we're not to have contact with the palace staff!" stuttered Abigail, backing away from the Duke. "The people are to be kept separate!"

The Duke raised his eyebrows in concern over her distress. "I wasn't aware of this decree!"

Abigail nodded emphatically. "The people are to stay in the garden, and the staff in the palace."

The Duke relaxed at her response and tried to put her at ease. "Well then, you mustn't fret. You have not left the garden. I haven't been commanded to stay out. We've done nothing wrong."

Abigail shook her head and whispered, "Something doesn't feel right about this."

The Duke held up his hands, slowly backing away from Abigail. "I never meant to worry you. I wanted only to meet the people the King speaks so highly of. But if it makes you feel uncomfortable, I'll leave."

Abigail was torn as she watched him walk casually away. The Duke was intriguing; maybe she was making a big deal out of nothing. Maybe the King's command had simply been not to enter the palace to speak with the staff. Maybe he'd never instructed them to avoid the palace staff entirely. Feeling foolish for her reaction, Abigail called out after the retreating Duke. "I'm sorry! I think I over-reacted! Why don't you come back and we can chat?"

The Duke grinned as he waved. "I'll leave you alone for today. Maybe some other time." He sauntered away with a final wave over his shoulder. "Enjoy the view," he called back to her.

Abigail sat down again, wanting to enjoy the view, but she was distracted and couldn't focus. *What had the King really said? Why were the people and the palace staff to be kept separate?* she wondered.

Abigail had never considered the idea of restriction before. Though she'd known the rule, there had never been an opportunity for it to be broken so it hadn't seemed hard to keep. Now, having been presented with the possibility that keeping the rule would make her give up something that appeared intriguing, Abigail found herself questioning it.

Both curiosity and unease danced inside her. A thought that had never entered her mind now surfaced: was the King keeping something from them?

Irritated, but resigned to the fact that the day would not turn out as she'd imagined, Abigail headed back to the gardens. "What an unusual day," she mused. "Perhaps I should find Theodore and discuss this with him."

The people were entering the central park as Abigail returned from the hill. She stretched up onto her tiptoes, hoping to spot Theodore's distinguishing silver hair in the crowd. Instead, her eyes caught Marc's as he made his way toward her. Gripped with a sudden urge to share her secret, Abigail waited impatiently for him to come close, then pulled his head down to whisper in his ear, "I just came back from exploring a hill I discovered near the edge of the garden." She intended to continue, only to have Marc interrupt her.

"What's the secret in that?" he questioned. Seeing her impatience, he quickly amended, "I'd love to come and see it with you, though."

Abigail shook her head. "That's not the secret, silly! While I was up there I met someone new!"

Marc furrowed his brow apprehensively. "No one

new has awakened in quite a while, Abigail. Who are you talking about?"

Abigail saw the King's eagle soaring overhead and knew the King wouldn't be far behind. She needed to join the singers, but before hurrying off, she quickly whispered, "Come find me after the performances."

Marc nodded before retreating to assemble with the warriors.

Surrounded by the choir, Abigail watched the King enter the clearing. It was time to begin. Opening her mouth to sing, Abigail felt the King's gaze rest upon her. For the first time, his smile stirred something different inside her. She felt exposed. Abigail looked away as she sang.

CHAPTER 4

Marc and Abigail scurried up the hill, bursting with excitement. They hadn't been able to get away from the others for several days so their secret had been forced to remain buried for a time. At first Abigail had been frustrated by the delay, but she'd soon realized it worked in her favour. Marc, who had also understood that the people and the palace staff were to be kept separate, was, at first, leery about the whole situation. But by now his curiosity was rampant, and he was willing to reason away his concerns about the meeting. That is the way of things when secrets stay buried. Curiosity grows and desire seeks to uncover.

Panting from excitement and exhaustion, Marc and Abigail ran to the top of the hill. The view didn't disappoint.

Marc gasped, rubbing his eyes.

"Oh, Abigail! This is far better than you described!" He shook his head in wonder. "Look at the palace! It's almost too bright to look at! It's glowing like fire! If the clouds floating around it didn't dim its brightness, we'd have to look away!"

Marc settled down on the grass, transfixed by the view. Abigail appreciated the beauty of the sight but still found herself glancing around restlessly. The panorama before her, though stunning, was not really why she'd come. The excitement of seeing the Duke again was what pulled her back.

"Do you think he'll come today?" she questioned Marc.

Marc shrugged. After seeing the palace, his desire to see the Duke had diminished. His misgivings were back in full force and he grimaced slightly as he responded.

"I don't know, Abigail. Maybe we should just enjoy the view for a while, and then leave. I think we need to talk to Theodore and find out what he thinks before we do something big like talk with the Duke. Theodore has been awake a lot longer than we have so he's much wiser. He'll know what to do."

Abigail rolled her eyes in disgust. "I knew you'd back out!" She huffed and stomped around in a circle. "I should have talked to Seth or Drew about this, instead of you!"

Marc bristled at the mention of his friends. "Leave them out of it," he snapped. "I'm just as capable of knowing what to do as they are!" Marc stood to his feet and stalked away from Abigail. "Forget it! Keep your secrets to yourself from now on!" He muttered over his shoulder as he stomped down the hill.

Abigail picked up a clump of dirt and threw it at Marc's retreating back, then kicked the ground in frustration. Marc had ruined everything! She sat on the hill, blind to the beauty before her, stewing over her situation. She'd wanted Marc to meet the Duke. But more than that, she'd wanted to see the Duke again, herself. Now it didn't seem like either would happen today.

Feeling like waiting any longer would be pointless, she got up to leave. That's when she caught sight of the anticipated figure in the distance. It was the Duke!

Her heart skipped a beat. Throwing caution to the wind, she called out to get his attention. She watched him turn, and pick up his pace when he recognized her. Her heart beat faster as Nachash strode toward her.

"Hello, Duke Nachash! I just happened to be out here enjoying the view when I saw you and thought I'd say hello," Abigail gushed, far too eagerly.

"I'm glad you called me over. After your reaction the last time we met, I didn't think I'd see you again."

Abigail flushed in embarrassment. "I'm sorry about being so silly last time. I was surprised by our encounter and didn't know how to respond."

"Don't worry about it," the Duke smiled. "I was so eager to meet one of the people, I never stopped to think about how you'd feel about meeting me."

Abigail and the Duke walked beside each other in silence for a while before he admitted somewhat self-consciously, "You know, I was probably just as excited as you were the other day. My greatest desire has always been to meet one of you."

Abigail relaxed at the Duke's confession. "Surely, having served the King, meeting the people would seem inconsequential," she half-teased the Duke.

Nachash shook his head emphatically. "Not at all! With all the wonder that surrounds him, the King still holds his people in very high regard. He speaks of you often."

"With that beautiful palace, these breathtaking gardens, and staff like you working for him, the King still speaks of us?" Abigail questioned incredulously.

"All the time. And not just to us!" exclaimed the Duke.

"If not just the staff, who else would he be talking with?" smiled Abigail, thinking the Duke would tease her with tales of talking animals or some such thing.

The Duke glanced at her in surprise. "Why, the Crown Prince of course! The two of them spend most of their time huddled away in the upper chambers under the wings of the eagle, speaking about their plan."

Abigail stopped walking to stare at the Duke. She had never heard of a Prince, and she was pretty sure none of the other people had either. Why had the King never spoken about him? And what was this plan the Duke spoke of? Abigail couldn't help but wonder what else the King was keeping from them.

Abigail spoke her questions out loud, confused. "I don't understand why he would keep all of this from us."

"I don't know either, Abigail," confessed the Duke. "The King won't share details of the plan with anyone. He says we just need to watch it unfold. I didn't mean to upset you by talking about the Prince. I assumed you knew about him."

Abigail felt bewildered. Until that moment, life had been simple. Now it seemed less so. "Do you know that, before today, I never realized there were things I didn't know? I knew the people, I knew the King, and I knew my purpose. I thought that was all there was to know. But now you tell me there is much I don't know."

"Well," mused the Duke, "he is the King, after all. He likely feels the need to keep some knowledge for himself. He shares with us what we need to know in order to fulfill our duties."

"What do you mean, 'fulfill our duties'?" questioned Abigail, increasingly upset.

The Duke smiled benevolently. "Abigail, surely you've thought about this before. How do you spend your days? What do you do?"

She shrugged, strangely embarrassed to admit it to the Duke. "We practise in the morning and perform in the afternoon. In between, we're free to explore the gardens and do as we wish."

The Duke nodded. "And what do you practise and perform?"

"I am a singer, so for me and some others, it's music. For some of the people it is gardening, for others it is wisdom. And then there are the warriors."

The Duke held Abigail's gaze until she felt uncomfortable. "What?" she blurted out more forcefully than she intended.

Nachash shrugged non-committedly. "It's nothing, really. I was just wondering, having never met any of the other people, if you have any say in the matter."

"What do you mean?" huffed Abigail.

"Well, did you decide you wanted to sing, or was it declared that you were a singer? Must you always sing, or can you change your mind and sing one day and garden another?" questioned the Duke.

Abigail was mystified. "I don't know! I've never thought about this before."

"If you are even half as intelligent as you are beautiful, I'm sure you would have thought of it eventually," the Duke consoled her. "And to be honest, it's taken me a long time to get where I am now. You're obviously younger than I am, so don't feel bad."

Abigail blushed at the Duke's compliment. "You say it's taken you time to get to where you are now. Where are you now?" she questioned.

The Duke gazed at her for a while before looking off into the distance. "Having served the King as long as I did, I started to see him differently. I saw how everything was always about him. The King and the Prince would meet in the upper chambers, apart from all of us, and plan and discuss. And I'd wonder, what is it they're planning? How to keep all of us under their control? How to keep us at our duties? Did they strategize ways to keep us from asking questions?"

The Duke's voice trailed off into silence. He seemed unaware of Abigail's presence. Then Nachash pulled his eyes back to Abigail's and continued solemnly, "I left the palace. Now I spend most of my time in the land beyond the garden."

Abigail was shocked by what he'd revealed. "There is

a land beyond the garden?" she asked, devastated by this last bit of revelation.

The Duke saw how upset she was and nodded sympathetically.

Overcome with all she had learned, Abigail placed her hand on his arm. "Thank you for sharing all this with me," she said softly. "You've shared your deepest thoughts and, in turn, given me much to think about."

Nachash squeezed her hand lightly with a sheepish grin. "You're so easy to talk to. I fear that in my excitement at meeting the people, I've made a fool of myself, exposing my deepest thoughts."

Struck with a sudden idea, Abigail grabbed his hand. "Why don't you come with me and meet some of the other people!" she exclaimed. "I know they'd enjoy your company as much as I have. I think they'd be just as shocked as I am to find out all that you know."

"Oh, I don't know," he shook his head doubtfully. "It's probably too soon. You remember how you reacted when you first saw me," the Duke teased.

Abigail laughed at the reminder and tugged at his hand. "Come on, you'll love meeting the people."

"Maybe I'll come tomorrow in between your practice and performance," suggested the Duke. "I really should get back to my men."

"Your men?" Abigail blurted. Her head was already spinning, and there was still more! "You have men with you? Where do they live? What do they do?"

The Duke blushed, seemingly embarrassed to answer her questions at first. But when she insisted, he humbly admitted, "I do have men. They live with me in what they've called the Land of Nachash. We spend our time doing what we want. Released from the burden of serving the King, we're free to search out our heart's desires and pursue them. It's actually a great place," he conceded. "There are no constraints placed upon us and we live for ourselves."

The Duke chucked her lightly on the cheek. "You, though, are unlike anyone I have ever met. Beautiful and kind, you've drawn out my innermost thoughts and secrets. Someone like you could keep me from my men forever." He winked at her before setting off.

Abigail pressed her hand to her burning cheek as she savoured his compliments. Never before had anyone made her feel the way she did when he touched her cheek or when he winked at her! Her head whirled with all he'd revealed. She felt special knowing he trusted her enough to bear his heart.

Suddenly excited to tell the people all she had learned, Abigail ran back to the gardens. But when she arrived at the central meeting place, she saw that the people were leaving. She was surprised to realize that she had missed the afternoon performance.

No person, ever, had missed this time with the King.

Excitement turned to fear. Abigail panicked, searching desperately for Theodore in the crowd. What had she done? Being with the Duke had been so exciting that she hadn't seen the eagle. She hadn't remembered the King.

Abigail needed to organize her thoughts so that she could be coherent if she found Theodore. Slowing her frantic searching, Abigail thought back on her time with the Duke and summoned forth a new confidence. What if today was the start of something new? Maybe, like the Duke, she was on a journey that would free her from what she'd never realized had been a burden.

Abigail raised her head high. She would not cower in shame. She did not regret her choice.

*****

The Duke and his followers watched Abigail through the darkness of the trees at the edge of the garden. Nachash warmed with the sensation of pride. This was going much better than he'd anticipated. She was far more delightful than he had expected her to be, and he loved how she had hung onto his every word. His followers clapped him on the back. They hadn't thought it would be this easy.

CHAPTER 5

Marc grabbed Abigail's arm from behind, whirling her around. "Where've you been? You missed the performance!" He was worried on her behalf, so he warned her, "Abigail, no one has ever missed an afternoon performance before. Theodore is very upset!"

Abigail jerked her arm away from Marc's grasp and raised her chin a notch higher. "I spent a lovely afternoon with the Duke. I'll have you know I *chose* not to attend the performance." It was only a half-truth, but she wished now it was the full truth.

Marc gave her a gentle shake. "Abigail, come to your senses. You're talking crazy! We don't *choose* to perform, we simply perform. It's who we are."

Abigail arched her brow in question. "Really, Marc? Have you ever stopped to think about what you just said? I suspect the days of me 'simply performing' without questioning are in the past. You should've stayed with me, Marc; you would have found what the Duke had to say fascinating!"

Marc shook his head in concern. "I don't know what happened up on that hill, Abigail, but you don't seem like the same person. I didn't want to do this, but I'm going to tell Theodore about what you've been up to."

A niggle of doubt shot through Abigail but she feigned nonchalance. "Do what you want, Marc. I wasn't planning on keeping it a secret anyway. In fact, I invited the Duke to come by for a visit after tomorrow's practice to meet more of the people and to give them the chance to meet him. There's a whole world out there we know nothing about, Marc! Aren't you just the tiniest bit curious?"

Marc backed away from Abigail in confusion. "Aren't you just the tiniest bit scared?" he countered. "I'm sorry that I can't share in your excitement, Abigail. I just don't have a good feeling about this, and I didn't right from the start. It was a mistake to keep your secret instead of letting Theodore deal with it. I won't make that mistake twice."

Marc walked away, shaking his head. Abigail felt strangely forlorn as she made her way through the garden. All she'd heard from the Duke swirled in her head and she couldn't make sense of any of it. She brushed away a tear, determined not to let Marc spoil what had been a lovely afternoon. She decided not to worry about something she didn't know what to do with. Let Marc and Theodore stew; she would carry on as before.

As Abigail walked through the garden, a gentle stirring came over her. She recognized the summons; it was the call to meet with the King. Her heart quickened. She loved sitting alone with the King, basking in his love and attention. Immediately, Abigail turned to head towards the stream. She saw the great eagle already waiting, hovering over the waters. Longing to see the King and throw herself in his arms to pour out everything to him, she started to run.

Hopping over stones and branches, she hurried towards him. A sudden thought slowed her down. Would he know of her meeting with the Duke already? Surely he did. But wasn't that why she wanted to talk to him? Didn't she want to find out what the Duke's words meant and what she was supposed to do with this new information?

With each step forward, more accusing thoughts nipped at her heel. Her run slowed to a walk, and then she stopped altogether. She didn't want the King to shine his bright light over her afternoon with the Duke. What if he seemed disappointed? Worse yet, what if he warned her to have no contact with the Duke? For the first time since she'd awoken, there was something Abigail wanted to keep from the King. She wasn't ready to pull her new discovery from the shadows into the light.

Abigail approached the stream, creeping quietly until she was behind a thicket of bushes that sheltered her from sight. She peered through the branches. Should she go to him or should she sneak away? Abigail looked down, trying to decide what to do. When Abigail looked back up, she started in surprise. The King was looking through the thicket right at her. He stretched out his arms in invitation.

Oh, how she longed to run into them! They were the safest place she knew. Torn between fear and longing, Abigail waited. Fear won. Covering her mouth to stifle a cry, Abigail turned and ran from the outstretched arms.

Racing back to the meadow, she threw herself down onto the softness of the grass. Excitement, confusion, fear, and desire jumbled around inside her and made their way out through gulping sobs.

It can be hard to keep track of time when you're having a good cry, and so she didn't know how long she'd wept before she heard Theodore shouting her name.

Abigail sat up and rubbed the tears from her eyes. She saw Theodore hurrying towards her, and her three warrior friends were with him. Reaching the place were

Abigail sat, Theodore dropped down to his knees and pulled her into his embrace.

"My dear girl," Theodore crooned. "What is going on, and why wouldn't you have come to me earlier?" He stroked her hair lovingly, holding her close.

Missing the arms she'd earlier longed to feel around her, Abigail settled into Theodore's embrace. Hiccupping through her tears, Abigail poured out the whole story. Theodore listened without comment, and speared the warriors with a stern glance when they attempted to interrupt. Abigail reached the end of all that'd happened and settled back to look into Theodore's face.

"I didn't want to upset anyone. I don't even really know what I've done that's so bad, besides missing today's performance. But the truth is, Theodore, I can't stop thinking about what the Duke said. As much as I love the King and have loved performing for him, when I really think about it, did I just do it because I didn't have a choice? Do any of us have a choice? And if we do, is this what we would choose?"

Theodore ran a hand through his hair subconsciously, standing it up on end. His eyes were as wild as his hair, and they darted back and forth between Abigail and the warriors as he contemplated what he'd heard. The warriors, who'd seemed so sure of Abigail's guilt before, were now sitting in silent deliberation, as confused as Theodore.

Seth broke the silence with his usual diplomacy. "Theodore, why don't you head back to your desk and search the scrolls. See what they say regarding palace staff and the people. See what they say about the Prince and a plan. As for the rest of us, why don't we get some rest, then see what tomorrow brings? Maybe the Duke won't even show up. If he does, we'll have the opportunity to see and hear for ourselves what Abigail has shared with us."

The group nodded in agreement, and though they went their separate ways, they all shared the experience of a restless night's sleep. They fought through their dreams, alternatively wrestling against, and then giving in to the pull they remembered from their earliest moments of awakening. A pull between earth and sky, light and dark.

Morning came earlier than anyone wanted and, although they went through the motions of practise, there was no passion, creativity, or sense of wonder. Duty was a heavy burden that morning.

When they finally met in the meadow, they were a surly lot. Some of the people had followed them, sensing something was happening. But they weren't aware of the turmoil that gripped Theodore, Abigail, and the warriors. They saw only silent frustration.

Abigail waited in silence, refusing to meet her friends' eyes. It stretched long and was more uncomfortable than anything she'd ever known. Frustration boiled up in her, and she was ready to walk away when she felt a rhythmic pounding.

It increased in sound and intensity, breaking the silence. Staccato beats drummed a fanfare and built into a crescendo culminating in the silhouette of a man on a horse breaking through the forest growth. He rode from the shadows, carried into the meadow on rays of afternoon sun as the people gaped in astonishment.

The instant Abigail felt the beat of the horse's hooves, her heart picked up the rhythm. She'd found the Duke handsome before, but nothing prepared her for the sight of him astride a magnificent black horse. The people didn't use animals in this manner, so seeing this display of power for the first time drew them to the Duke. The whole garden throbbed with his entrance. Soon people from all corners of it trailed to the meadow where the Duke and his horse ambled across waving grasses and flowers, a stream of spectators trickling behind them.

Though all eyes were on him, the Duke had eyes only for Abigail. Nachash stopped his horse several feet in front of her and jumped from its back. He covered the short distance between them in long, confident strides.

"I could hardly wait to see you again," he murmured, leaning close. Abigail's temperature soared as the Duke brushed a kiss into the palm of her hand before straightening to acknowledge the people. "Abigail, please introduce me to these people! I'm eager to meet them!"

The moments that followed were a blur as Abigail led Nachash through the crowd, making introductions. She breathed out words as best she could over the erratic flutter in her chest, but how was she supposed to focus when the Duke never let go of her hand? He held onto her with a possessive air that made her feel singled out, special in a very different way.

By the time they reached Theodore and her warrior friends, the mysterious Duke had completely captured the people's imagination. He bowed low before Theodore.

"You are obviously the wise man I have heard so much about," Nachash spoke respectfully. "Your wisdom is known throughout the palace."

Theodore felt flustered by the Duke's effusive praise. The bowing made him uncomfortable. *Yet, this is not an altogether unpleasant feeling*, he thought.

Nachash turned to Abigail. "Would you mind terribly, if I left you for a time to speak with this distinguished gentleman and his friends?" he asked, motioning to include the three warriors.

Abigail nodded, yet felt somewhat bereft as he let go of her hand and strolled off, chatting with the men. But she wasn't alone for even a moment. As soon as the Duke was out of hearing range, the women crowded around with eager questions.

"What's it like to have such a handsome man completely enamored with you?"

"How did you meet him? He's so mysterious!"

"How could you bear to let him go?"

Abigail tried to take in the women and their questions but she was distracted from their words by what she saw in their eyes. She had something they wanted.

The people had never looked at each other in relation to one another. They'd always seen their worth by looking to the King, who saw each one as an individual, a masterpiece. Yet, as she basked in the adoration of the Duke and the envy of the women, she looked through fresh eyes.

None of the other women had been fashioned quite as well as she had. It was just as the Duke had said; she really was the most beautiful. And in that moment of realization, she saw that the other women knew it, too. How could their admiration not turn to envy and her astonishment to pride?

The Duke returned to Abigail near the time of the afternoon performance. "Thank you, Abigail, for giving me the gift of meeting the people," he smiled. "It was an unsurpassed delight for which I am grateful." Tilting his head closer, he continued, "The time has come for me to leave. I don't want to interrupt your afternoon performance."

Loath to see him go, Abigail blurted out, "Come with me and watch."

The Duke's eyes flashed and his jaw clenched ever so slightly before he responded softly, "Thank you for the invitation, but I really need to go. Your focus is the King and I wouldn't want to take any attention away from him."

She blushed as she whispered, "I would love for you to hear me sing."

The Duke smiled and gave one of her curls a gentle tug. "I want that, too. Maybe someday, when the time is right." He jumped on his horse and rode off without a backward glance.

CHAPTER 6

Theodore poured over the scrolls again, looking for answers. He couldn't find any references to palace staff being kept separate from the people. The only restriction on the people that he could see was that they were not to leave the garden or enter the palace. He did find references to the Prince and to a plan, but they seemed vague. Frustrated with his search, Theodore rolled up the scrolls and tossed them in a jar.

Grabbing a fresh scroll, he decided to focus on the people instead of the King. Theodore began jotting down changes he'd observed among the people over the past weeks since the Duke had entered the garden.

Theodore scribbled down random points before

teasing out common threads. There was a growing sense of discontent among the people. Conversations were frequently characterized by an unwillingness to continue with things the way they had always been. In the weeks since the Duke's arrival, the people had grown in their knowledge and understanding. This was having a direct impact on their practise and performance. They no longer worked with the same focus or enthusiasm. Attendance was sporadic at best. The people spoke far more about their journeys of self-discovery than they did of the King. And they never spent time remembering their moment of awakening anymore.

The more Theodore thought about it, the more weary he felt recalling all the endless babble about 'self.' But what sickened him the most was admitting that he was prone to the same. When a rare moment of silence emerged, he attempted to fill it with stories of himself, easily frustrated if someone beat him to it.

His scribbles revealed another trend. There was a growing tendency to ignore the royal summons. Even he was guilty of it. The summons had been hard to ignore at first, but the more often he did it, the easier it got. When he'd questioned the people about why they were ignoring the royal summons, they explained that it freed them up to explore areas of interest besides the King.

They were right. Theodore had found that exploring

his talent for writing had opened up new and interesting avenues. He chuckled as he remembered the poem he'd recited to the people yesterday. It'd been a silly verse that poked fun at the gardeners. It had everyone laughing. Well, everyone except the gardeners, but they always did have an underdeveloped sense of humour

Skimming what he'd written, Theodore threw his pen down in disgust. He read of joy become burden, love become smothering, and boundaries of protection now standing as barriers to adventure. Innocence was withering and being replaced by the seed of doubt.

Theodore pounded his desk in frustration. He was one of people's leaders! If he didn't know what to do, how could he lead his people? Feeling the pull again, he looked through his window and saw the eagle hovering above the stream. His anger poured over and he pushed back his chair and marched towards the stream. Seeing the King sitting on a smooth rock, waiting, Theodore unleashed all the hostility that had built up over the past weeks.

"How am I supposed to lead this people when I myself don't know what to do?" he shouted at the King. "I come to you when I don't understand, and you speak to me in riddles! I'm the wisest of the wise ones, and yet you won't help me to understand. I won't bear this burden of leadership any longer if you don't give me some answers! What is happening to me? What's happening to the people?"

Spent from his angry tirade, Theodore slumped against a rock, holding his head in his hands. A gentle hand lifted his head so that he looked into the eyes of the King.

"Why do you bear burdens you weren't meant to carry?" questioned the King.

Theodore shook his head in confusion. "You always speak in riddles. I don't understand."

"Who asked you to lead this people? Did I give you that responsibility? Are they *your* people?"

Looking into the eyes of the King, Theodore felt clarity settle around him. He laughed self-consciously. "No, you never did. I guess after speaking with the Duke, I kind of took the responsibility upon myself. He seemed to think that I was the leader of the people, and I never corrected him."

"So, don't worry about leading the people. That's my job. Do what I made you to do," replied the King.

Theodore saw the unconditional love and acceptance in the King's eyes, and continued, "I was made to think on you, write about you, and speak about you." Theodore paused before continuing. "Forgive me for asking, but why must the focus of everything always be on you?"

"Who would you rather focus on?" probed the King.

Theodore shrugged non-committedly. "I don't know that I have anything or anyone specifically in mind."

The King gazed off into the distance as he responded. "I've never ordered you, or anyone else for that matter, to focus solely on me. Of all creation, I fashioned you to be most like me. You're made to respond to me, to long for me. I'm the King and the glory is mine."

Theodore prickled. "Why do you need all the glory? The Duke says it's because you're egotistical, selfish, desiring to keep good from us, requiring us to deny ourselves for your benefit. Why can't we share the glory with you?"

Voicing his deepest thoughts empowered Theodore to continue. "Look at Abigail. She is breathtakingly beautiful, yet you kept that from her. Look at Seth, Drew, and Marc. They are by far the most skilled warriors in the Kingdom, yet it took the Duke to point it out to all of us. Look at me! No one is as wise as I am! No one! Yet, you've never elevated me to the status I've earned, the place I deserve."

The King stood, indicating that their meeting was coming to a close. "Theodore, who made you wise? What good do you suppose would come from elevating you to the status you think you deserve? I never kept Abigail's beauty from her or anyone else; it's on display for all to see and enjoy. While she has one form of beauty, other women carry another. Who gave it to them? What purpose would there be in elevating her form over the other's? Do you think Abigail will grow lovelier from focusing on herself and her beauty?

And what of the warriors? For whom are their skills best used, Theodore? Do you understand all that I made, why I made it, and the purpose that is yet to be achieved? I don't *need* all the glory; I simply have all the glory. I am the King. All that you see, all that you are—it came from me and is an expression of my character."

The King seemed more resigned than angry, but still Theodore cowered slightly as he finished. "Theodore, I made you and I know you inside and out. I know the way to your greatest joy and fulfillment. But this is something you must learn for yourself."

The King turned to leave, then paused, "Theodore, let the people know the afternoon performances have come to an end. I'll be in the central meeting place each afternoon and anyone is welcome to come join me there, but no one is required."

The King walked back towards the palace under the spread of the great eagle's wings.

Theodore walked back to his cottage with a heavy spirit. He informed each person he encountered that there would be no more formal practice or performance. He was hesitant to share the news at first, fearful of the people's reaction, but he quickly saw that most of the people were relieved, grateful to be freed from a burden.

Back at the cottage, he slumped at his desk. Reading

through the scrolls of the King again, he was reminded of who the King was. Tears trickled down his cheeks as a feeling of loss crept in with the shadows.

CHAPTER 7

Abigail ran to the meadow in hopeful anticipation. Nachash hadn't said for sure if he would come for a visit today, but how she hoped he would! She was surprised by the strength of her attraction to him. Nothing and no one stirred excitement in her like the Duke did. Every time she looked at him, her heart beat a little faster and she couldn't tear her eyes away, scared she'd miss his glance in her direction.

And when he did look at her, it wasn't enough. Then she would long for his whispers, his touch, and his smile in a way that almost made her crazy. This tumultuous, craving kind of passion was so different than what she'd felt for the King. With the King, she'd never worried about the things that consumed her now. The King spread his love around the people and it had always felt like multiplication rather than division. What she felt for the Duke was opposite. Every look he cast towards another woman sparked a fire of jealously that licked at her insides, scorching her pride, burning her self-confidence.

When she heard the familiar beat of a horse's hooves, she ran towards the sound. "Nachash, you came," she breathed. "I hadn't seen you for a couple of days and missed you!"

The Duke slid from his horse, kissing her absently on the cheek. He was different today. Long looks were replaced with restless pacing. Lazy whispers for short answers.

Wanting to placate him, Abigail tugged on his arm. "Let's go for a walk around the garden," she coaxed. "You know, get away from everyone else for a bit." She lowered her eyes, peering up at him through her eyelashes in what she knew was a tempting vision.

He glanced her way for a quick second before shrugging her off. "I'm tired of walking around the gardens. Actually, Abigail, I came today to tell you and the men that I won't be back for a while."

Abigail recoiled at the unexpected announcement. "Nachash, what do you mean?" She wanted to keep the desperation from her voice but knew it saturated every syllable. "Please, Nachash, you know we all look forward to your visits, but it's different for me. The seconds drag when you're gone even more than they fly when you're here."

The Duke threw his hands up in frustration. "Don't you ever wonder what's beyond these walls?" he ground out. "There's a whole world out there, a land they've named after me and you never seem interested in it. I come to see you in your garden; don't you want to come see me in my land?"

Abigail grabbed hold of his arm in a futile attempt to pin him down as he continued his rant. "It's beautiful here, I'll give you that, but I thought you'd long for more excitement and adventure than just these walls." He gestured to the high stone walls surrounding the garden. "If you never leave, don't you think you'll always wonder about what's beyond them?"

Nachash stopped pacing and grabbed her arms, pulling her close. "You are so beautiful, and there's very little I want as much as I want time with you," he admitted. "But, Abigail, I can't spend forever coming here to this garden just to walk around it for a while with you. I want a life with you." He leaned closer to whisper, "I want all of you."

She shivered with delight, having him so near. Hearing his desire for her brought about a heady feeling that set her mind spinning. But to her frustration, she couldn't escape the constant pull between the exciting newness of being with the Duke, and the reassuring calmness of what she'd always known in the garden with the King.

"Oh, Nachash," she breathed. "You know what Theodore read in the scrolls. We can't leave the garden. It's the only restriction the King has placed upon us." Abigail longed for him to understand her predicament.

The Duke dropped his hands from her arms in resignation. "And so you choose to stay and serve the King," he muttered, walking away. "I offer you everything and you give it up for him."

"Don't leave!" Abigail wailed, running after him. She grabbed him around the waist and spun him around, clinging to him.

"Please don't go," she begged shamelessly. "I can't bear to lose you! Things are different now. None of the people go to perform for the King anymore. We're becoming more like you, seeking after our own desires rather than catering to his."

"You don't see it," Nachash rasped. "The King says he keeps nothing from you, but have you met his son, the Prince? No! Are you free to leave the garden? NO! You are bound to the garden and to your servitude to him."

He ran angry fingers through his hair. "Were you mine, I'd keep nothing from you. I wouldn't make you serve me; I'd free you to do whatever you pleased. I have a whole Kingdom of men who live this way, free to do as they please, to be who they wish to be, and to be with the one they want to be with."

Abigail reeled with what he had said. She leaned against his chest, hoping the steady beat of his heart would anchor her whirling mind. In the Kingdom, no person belonged to anyone else; they all belonged to the King. "You mean, in your land, men take women as their own?" she questioned incredulously.

Nachash rubbed her back. "Yes," he chuckled, "and some women take men to be their own."

"Why would people belong to each other?" questioned Abigail.

"How do you feel when you see me talking to other women or smiling at them, Abigail?"

Her cheeks burned red. She knew he was aware of her jealously. He quickly soothed her. "Don't worry, I'm not upset. I feel the same way when I see you talking to those three warrior friends of yours or when I think about the fact that they get to hear you sing."

Abigail looked up at him in surprise. "Why, Nachash, you know they're just my friends. I don't feel the same way about them as I do about you. Besides, I don't sing for them. I sing for the King."

Anger flared in the Duke's eyes. "You don't need to remind me of that, darling. I remember all too well who you sing for," he spat out. "I assure you, Abigail, if you came with me to my Kingdom, I wouldn't share you with anyone."

A wave of pleasure washed over Abigail as the Duke made his intentions clear. But it changed to apprehension with his next words: "I need to go speak with the warriors now, Abigail. We have some plans to discuss. I won't be back for another week or so. When I come back, it will be the last time. On that day, you'll need to make your choice."

Abigail clutched at his shirt but he pulled her hands free and jumped on his horse. As he whirled it around, the magnificent beast reared up, tossed its mane, then galloped away. The Duke's final offer floated back on the breeze, "If you really want to live, come, join me."

CHAPTER 8

Abigail rubbed her eyes, trying to wipe away the evidence of a sleepless, tear-filled night as she stumbled to Theodore's cottage. She wanted to feel composed so she knocked with authority. The door swung open and one glimpse of Theodore's weary countenance caused her to break down.

"Oh, Theodore," she sobbed. "You look as bad as I feel. Why do we have to choose? Nachash has given me an ultimatum, it's him or the King. How do I choose? Why won't the King let me have both? His rules are tearing us apart."

Theodore squeezed Abigail's shoulder and drew her in. He unconsciously shot a glance towards the stream where he'd met with the King the day before, then shut the door behind Abigail. Theodore led Abigail to a chair then lowered himself down on the chair beside her, shaking his head sadly. "The Duke has given the warriors . . . well, all the people, really, the same ultimatum. It's him or the King, he says."

"What do we do?" moaned Abigail. "Life as we've known it is forever changed, whatever we choose."

Theodore nodded. "It's as I feared at the start of all this upheaval. If we choose to stay, we'll always wonder what it would've been like if we'd left. If we go . . ." Theodore's voice trailed off. He shuddered before continuing. "The only rules imposed on us are that we are not to enter the palace or to leave the gardens. I fear the wrath of the King if we choose to leave."

"Nachash could return any day, forcing us to choose."

Theodore nodded silently then stood and led Abigail to the door. "It's time for you to leave, Abigail. There's much I must ponder."

"You have a plan, don't you?" questioned Abigail.

"I do. You may not like it, but I'm one of the wise ones for a reason, and I do what I feel I must. I'm going to the King."

Abigail gasped. "Theodore, no! Don't tell him about the Duke. You'll ruin everything!"

Theodore gazed at Abigail sadly. "No, my child, I don't believe it's I alone who have ruined things."

Abigail crossed her arms defensively. "Are you blaming me for this? Really, Theodore, I would have thought it was beneath you to cast stones."

"Abigail, something has been set in motion that is larger than you or I. I feel like we have a choice in the outcome, somehow, but no, I don't blame you. Perhaps it is the Duke that I blame."

"You're jealous of him," spat Abigail. "He's a threat to your power and you want it back!"

Theodore shook his head as he turned away from Abigail and back to his desk. "What's coming has already begun. I'll go to the King." He looked back at Abigail before she closed the door. "Though somehow, I suspect he already knows."

Abigail yanked the door closed behind her. She needed to find the warriors. Surely they'd see things differently than Theodore. Surely they'd stop him from involving the King.

Abigail hadn't walked far when she saw a familiar trio ambling down a nearby path. Picking up her skirts, she ran to catch up to Seth, Drew, and Marc.

"Abigail. We were just talking about you," Drew commented when Abigail was in hearing distance.

"Are you blaming me for everything, too?" she snapped.

"Relax, Abigail," cautioned Seth. "We were merely discussing our latest conversation with the Duke." Seth eyed her carefully before continuing. "The Duke is tired of his visits to the garden. He says they've come to an end."

Abigail nodded as Drew picked up where Seth left off. "He invited us to come live in the land beyond the gardens."

"What are you thinking?" questioned Abigail softly.

Seth answered slowly. "He fills our minds with stories of the land beyond. We'd be lying if we said we weren't curious."

"But?" probed Abigail.

"The people all know that if we leave, we break the command the King has given us. The consequences will be big." Seth worried his lip as he gazed off in the direction of the palace. "I fear that if we choose the Duke, we lose the King."

"You're at least entertaining the thought of leaving, though, aren't you?" Abigail grabbed Seth's arm and forced him to look her in the eye. "Seth, will you leave?"

Seth shook her off. "It's foolishness to even entertain the thought . . ." his voice trailed off.

Abigail turned to Marc and Drew. "You haven't said anything. What are your thoughts?"

Marc grinned. "You know how Nachash rides that horse? He says that in the land beyond the garden, his land, there are all sorts of animals. Wild animals. His men tame the animals. They ride them and they race them! Can you imagine?" His eyes sparkled at the thought of adventure.

Drew chimed in, "Nachash speaks of days centered on ourselves. He says all they do in his land is live each day exactly how they choose to." Drew leaned in closer and spoke softly, in wonder, "The Duke says that his land is characterized by competition."

Abigail drew back in confusion. "What's that?"

"I know, I asked the same thing." Drew continued, growing animated in the explanation. "Competition is when two or more people do the same activity and the better one is chosen."

"Who decides who is better?" queried Abigail, skeptically.

"It must be the Duke," spoke Drew. "You know, just like he was the one to decide you were the most beautiful girl in the garden." Drew gave Abigail a teasing shove.

Abigail blushed. "Don't be silly."

Marc laughed at her discomfort. "You don't seem to mind when Nachash points it out," he chortled.

"It sounds like you're seriously considering the change." Abigail was somewhat astonished to realize there was a pull to the Duke among more of the people than just herself. "Theodore's going to summon a meeting with the King," warned Abigail. "I don't think it is a good idea!"

Seth contradicted her confidently. "It's exactly what we need to do. We must gather all the people and go to the King." He held up his hand to stop the barrage of questions that threatened to spill from each of his friends. "If we decide to go through with the change, it would be ludicrous to do so without all the information. In fact, I'll go to Theodore immediately. We don't have much time to waste."

Abigail shrugged, feigning nonchalance, but her frustration was evident. "I just don't think this is something we need to involve the King in."

Seth pierced her with a look that reminded her eerily of Theodore. "Abigail," he spoke, "I believe the King is already very involved in this matter." He turned from the group and set off down the path to Theodore's cottage.

Abigail stood with Drew and Marc and watched him go. "What if we decide to leave, but Seth and Theodore decide to stay," whispered Abigail choking back tears. "I want so badly to be with the Duke, but I don't want to lose my friends."

Drew shook his head gravely. "I suspect, my dear, we'll each have to choose for ourselves."

****

Nachash watched from the shadows as Drew and Marc led Abigail home. He sniggered as the wind carried their words back to him. "I want the Duke, but I want my friends, too!" mimicked the Duke. "Someday very soon, you'll see, my lovely, that if you choose me, there will be nothing left." The Duke laughed cruelly. "You foolish people. You can't see that you've already chosen."

CHAPTER 9

With no time to waste, the meeting was set. The following afternoon the people shuffled towards the meeting place with an air of reluctance. When they arrived, rather than collect in an orderly fashion like they did for their performances, they lumped together into a huddled mass. Theodore examined the people and saw their uncertainty. He listened to them speak and heard belligerence in their voices. Deep foreboding wrapped around him like a cloak. Before leaving his cottage, he'd felt compelled to gather all his scrolls into a pouch and tie them around his waist. He now grasped the pouch as a measure of comfort as he wandered amongst the people, listening to their murmurings.

"The King had better not be upset about us not being

at afternoon performances!"

"He was the one who terminated them, after all! How could he be angry at us? We only obeyed, did as we were commanded to!"

"He's probably the one who tired of coming to hear us perform. I'm sure he stayed in the palace because he had something better to do and now he wants to pass the blame on to us!"

"He's always kept us on a short leash, forcing us to serve his every demand. When the Duke came and opened our eyes, the King probably got angry that the Duke spoiled things for him. He's probably sitting on his throne, sulking."

"Maybe he's not sulking! Maybe he and his supposed Prince have been plotting ways to get their power back. Maybe he called the meeting to dole out punishment. What if this is the day he squishes us under his thumb for good?"

The murmurings became increasingly hysterical and Theodore sought to appease the crowds by reminding them of the truth. "I was the one who called this meeting, not the King. We merely want to talk. You've seen the eagle above the central garden each day. You know what that means. It means the King was there waiting for us. He didn't stay in the palace, sulking on his throne. He doesn't tire of us. He was here every afternoon, waiting to meet with us!"

Though he tried to speak reason to the people,

Theodore could see they were not listening to him because they didn't want to hear what he was saying. To his surprise, he saw that many enjoyed the chaos, relished the malicious gossip against the King, and revelled in the possibility of confrontation. Theodore's insides churned as he realized his greatest fear had already been realized.

The people had already chosen and this meeting was only a formality. The day the Duke rode back into the garden, they would follow him out.

Knowing this to be true, Theodore had clarity for the first time since the change had begun. Knowing exactly what must not happen, Theodore was desperate to stop what seemed inevitable. He frantically scanned the crowd for his warrior friends. The time had come for them to use force and put an end to this nonsense. The days for passivity were behind them. Theodore knew they must act.

He spotted Seth, Drew, and Marc standing beside Abigail, observing the commotion. With no thought to propriety, he pushed his way through the people to join them. Finally reaching them, he sagged against Seth in relief.

"Seth, assemble the warriors! You must employ forceful methods of dissuasion. The people are speaking lies and malice against the King! They may go so far as to hurt him when he appears!"

Seth was about to respond when the steady beat of

the eagle's wings announced the coming of the King. The people's reaction to the sound looked so ridiculous that Theodore would have laughed had he not been terrified. People quickly sought shelter, moving to stand under large branches, huddling amongst shrubs, or crouching in groups, faces turned in. Their attempts to hide from the King were pitiful.

Silence descended over chaos with the heavy footfall, the swish of robes, the light of his presence. The King walked among them. Breath caught in Theodore's throat as he gazed upon his beauty.

The King turned and looked at Theodore, and Theodore felt crushed by the depth of pain reflected in the King's gaze. Feeling certain of what would transpire before the day's end, Theodore felt stooped by the magnitude of the moment. There was only one who could save them.

Running to the King, Theodore grabbed his arm. "Stop them!" Theodore pleaded. "They don't see! They don't understand what they are about to do!"

The King placed his hand gently overtop of Theodore's. "You're right, they don't. Theodore, what you see happening is as much beyond you as it's beyond all of them. My child, you, too, will leave."

Theodore clutched at the King desperately. "Please don't talk like this!" he nearly shouted. "I'll never leave you!"

The King ran his thumb down Theodore's cheek, tracing a trail of tears that mirrored his own. Then the King whispered urgently, "Theodore, you must not forget!" He placed Theodore's hand on his cheek and Theodore felt Kingly tears run through his fingers as the King spoke. "Don't forget how very much I love you." The King rested his forehead against Theodore's and closed his eyes. A shudder rippled through the mighty body of the King before he pulled himself away.

"It's time," he whispered.

Theodore wept as the King moved to the centre of the garden.

"My people," the King's voice resonated deeply. "I've missed our time together. I've waited at this very spot every afternoon, longing for you to join me. What keeps you from my presence?"

The uneasy silence was broken as the people murmured amongst themselves. Finally, a surly voice shouted out from the back of the crowd, "We simply didn't want to come. We've had far too much on our minds as of late. Besides, what gives you the right to demand we come entertain you each day?"

Theodore groaned at the belligerent comment. The King answered sadly, "Have I demanded your presence? I thought it was our mutual joy. Are you commanded to entertain me, or do we simply delight in each other?"

Marc stepped up and spoke courageously. "Duke Nachash has been here. We've gotten to know him, and have found we enjoy his company. He believes we are foolish to stay locked behind these walls, serving you mindlessly. You say to leave these walls is certain death. Nachash says to leave these walls is to truly live and be free."

The people murmured loud agreement as Marc spoke. Theodore watched the King carefully but saw that he was not surprised by Marc's confession; the King did not look angry or defeated, only sad.

The King nodded. "Yes, I've heard of his visits." Looking intently at the people, the King questioned them. "What do you suppose happens now?"

Theodore stepped forward and began to speak nervously. "My King," he asserted, "I have a proposal to present. Allow us to stay. Can't we have it both ways? Must our living arrangements be exclusive? Does it have to be the garden OR the Land of Nachash? Perhaps we could live here but travel to that land to visit and learn more of it."

The King's voice was soft but firm and he never wavered as he responded. "No, my children. I will not share. Do you presume to have surprised me or caught me off guard? Do you present me with plans that you suppose I could not have thought of?"

He continued his dialogue. "I knew this day was coming. I've heard your cries against me—how I have enslaved you, kept you in bondage, stifled you. Today you will answer me. No more will you remain unwillingly in the garden I created for you. Today you choose.

"I saw this day before I made you. I knew that one day you would long to leave this garden, to step beyond these walls." The King gestured emphatically as he spoke. "Look around you. Are any of the gates closed? Are there any locks to keep you in?" He continued, "You've always been free to leave if you choose. Do you think I would have allowed the Duke access had it not been part of my plan?"

As the people turned to look at the walls, they gaped at what had always been true but they had never seen. The gates were open. They were free to leave; they always had been.

As Abigail watched the proceedings, she grew increasingly unsettled by the intense pulling within. From the moment of awakening there had been a residual pull, but never had it felt as strong as it did now. The strain between light and dark. The push of music against silence. The ethereal pressing against the earthly.

She felt the gentle gaze of the King. She knew his love, his patience, and his kindness. But still the open gates beckoned. Still the words of the Duke whispered to her on the wind, his insinuations that there was much more than this. She tasted the tantalizing possibility that perhaps the King was keeping something from her, and that life beyond these walls held more than life within them.

The staccato rhythm of horse hooves sounded in the distance. Abigail's heart quickened at the now familiar sound. She glanced back when the King resumed speaking. "You've always been free to choose. Choose me! You've seen that I am gentle. I will never rule harshly. My reign is one of love and justice."

Against the rumbles of rebellion, the King spoke a final warning. "In the Land of Nachash, you will be free to serve yourselves, but you will find that in serving yourselves, you serve the Duke. He entices you now, wooing you with promises of freedom, but it is these very promises that will entangle you. It is the Duke who will enslave you! With him, not all is as it seems."

Quiet rebellion exploded into open revolution. "The King is jealous of the Duke! He speaks lies to turn us from the Duke. He attempts to steal our freedom, restrict our choice! All this talk of love is a lie! Love has no boundaries, no restrictions!" The mass of people moved as one angry flood headed for the open gates.

Bitter disappointment fed Abigail's mutiny. Yes, life had been wonderful in the garden, but that was before she'd considered who she was serving. It used to seem so natural. Now she heard the King clearly and he freely admitted that he was keeping something from them—he was stopping them from pursuing themselves with absolute abandon.

It made her sick.

The Duke rode up in time to hear the King finish and he wasted no time challenging the King. "You speak so poorly of me when it is I who offer them complete freedom" Nachash smirked.

The King held the Duke's gaze. "Nachash, let them choose, but don't hide the truth."

"I'm the one who invited them to freedom while you would keep them enslaved in the garden of servitude," answered the Duke.

The people started towards the gates and Abigail felt the Duke's eyes on her, encouraging her to join them. Excitement and pain mixed and churned inside. The time to choose had come. She started with slow, cautious steps when the powerful voice of the King stopped her in her tracks.

"If you leave through those gates, they won't stay open any longer; they'll lock behind you. In the Land of Nachash there is sickness and death that cannot enter my Kingdom. If you walk through those gates, you'll have to stay in that land until the way of return appears."

A hush fell over the people as the impact of the King's

words settled. They paused to look around the garden. They glanced at each other before looking between the Duke and the King. One they gazed at with ill-concealed longing, the other with a sad mix of nostalgia and regret.

The King's voice lowered with intensity. "Children, when you leave, don't forget me," he implored. "I won't leave you there. Watch for the way of return. I love you and have a plan for your rescue. The Prince will come to lead you home."

Theodore stumbled to the King in a panic. He'd known the outcome was sure; he'd known the people had already decided. But he could never have imagined the intense pain it would cause him to see the people stream towards the gates before the King had even finished speaking. They ran for freedom with barely a backward glance. Theodore fell on his knees before the King, choking on sobs. "Oh, King, if they leave, how do they come back? What will be the way to return?"

The King stroked Theodore's silvery mane gently. "Those who seek me will find me."

"Those who go won't know what to look for, what to listen for, my King!" wept Theodore.

"They must read the scrolls and watch for my son! I'll send him when the time is right," assured the King. Suddenly the King's tone became urgent. "Theodore, no one needs to leave! Everyone has a choice!"

Theodore tore his gaze from the King and looked around. The people ran for the gates with excitement, enticed by the promise of more.

CHAPTER 10

Theodore watched the people push through open gates while the promises of the King echoed around them. Didn't they see the gates closing slowly behind them? Didn't they care?

He cried out in desperation, "Stop! Think about what you're leaving!" He staggered for the gates, trying in vain to slow the departure of people from the Kingdom, but his pleas of desperation were drowned in raucous excitement.

Theodore wept in despair. No one listened.

A chorus of familiar voices jerked his head up in alarm. Marc and Drew were headed for the gates. Seth followed, gesturing frantically. It looked like he was trying to convince them to stay, but though he may have talked against leaving, he continued to walk with his friends. Theodore called to them but they couldn't hear over the commotion. Staggering through the maze of confusion, Theodore managed to catch up with the group of warriors. He grabbed hold of Seth's shirt and spun him around.

"Seth, this is madness! Where are you going?" Theodore was almost incoherent from weeping.

Seth was near panic himself. "Drew and Marc have made up their minds. They won't listen!" Seth wiped at his eyes and began pulling at Drew and Marc. "For goodness sake, listen to reason, men!" he implored.

"Seth!" Theodore shouted. "You can't follow them!"

Seth paused for a moment and eyed Theodore, tears streaming down his cheeks. "I can't let them go without me," he whispered.

"You'll never return," rasped Theodore.

"There will be a way. We'll watch for it, you and me," implored Seth.

Theodore jerked away from Seth, shaking his head. "No, never! This can't be happening."

Seth looked with longing for the last time at the Kingdom before following his friends through the open gates. His choice was made.

Theodore collapsed to his knees. People ran from the Kingdom without hesitation. They didn't spare even a glance for what they were leaving. The backs of the warriors faded into the distance and would soon slip from sight. To stay meant he would have the King, but to stay meant he would have only the King. There was no one else.

Theodore fixed his eyes on the King. Was he enough? Was Theodore willing to give up everyone he knew and life as he'd known it, to remain alone in the Kingdom with the King? He watched Abigail's curls bounce as she rode out on the back of the Duke's horse.

And he knew.

Shakily, Theodore rose to his feet. Step by step, leaden feet carried him forward. His walk switched to a run as he tried to catch up with the people he loved.

Theodore stumbled into the new land. He fell when his foot caught in an opening between some rocks. Pain tore through his foot as he wrenched it free and crawled forward. He didn't realize that the pouch he carried around his waist had caught between the stones. Unnoticed, it snapped loose and fell to the ground.

Knowing he had left the Kingdom and entered the Land of Nachash, Theodore convulsed, vomiting uncontrollably. Emptier than he'd ever been, Theodore rose to his feet and walked forward. His progress was not fast. He paused every couple of steps to look back at what he was leaving. He'd walked far enough that his beloved Kingdom was fading behind him. The gates were almost closed but Theodore could still see the King, standing, arms outstretched in invitation, observing their exile.

But Theodore knew he couldn't run back to the King and desert the people. This would be his final glimpse of the King. He watched the gates close firmly and completely.

The exile was complete.

Theodore had turned to continue his journey when a deep roaring filled his ears. He covered them, cowering in fear; what fresh terror was this? He gawked wildly at the people around him but they seemed oblivious to the sound, unable to hear. The ground shook beneath Theodore's feet as the roar reached a crescendo. Suddenly, the ground began to crumble, cratering inwards as dirt dropped away into the bowels of the earth.

Theodore scrambled away from the deepening chasm. Geysers of water surged from the deep gorge, wetting Theodore's face as it sprayed into the air, then dropped into a fast-moving river that wound around the Kingdom walls and gates. The waters came full circle and collided forcefully with each other, tumbling into the deep canyon. Soon the Kingdom was surrounded by a roaring sea.

Theodore watched as waves of water settled into the space between the garden walls and the new land. Churning breakers crashed against the ground near Theodore's feet. He ran from their reach as they carved jagged gashes across the dirt.

When their relentless progress was stayed, Theodore felt drawn to the waves in curiosity. He bent down and let them rush over his hands. All the water he'd known before this had been a bubbling brook or a gentle spring. He'd never seen water this angry or powerful. It's commanding breakers had eaten up the land and forced Theodore so far back that the Kingdom had virtually disappeared in the distance.

As surely as the waters covered the land, they drowned Theodore in despair. The sea appeared impassable and on the other side of it lay the Kingdom. These waters blocked any hope of return.

Theodore's thoughts were interrupted by a sudden surge of light that flashed from within the Kingdom, blinding in its intensity. Rubbing his eyes to clear black spots, he shook his head and looked across the waters once again. A bank of thick clouds obscured the opposite shore from sight. Hopelessness enveloped Theodore as completely as the clouds had enveloped the Kingdom. There would be no return until the King revealed the way.

At the edge of this new land, Theodore watched the past dissipate before his eyes. In deep anguish, he did all he knew to do. He called out to the King. He cried long and loud, and the sound echoed across the waters. As Theodore wept, the great eagle rose from behind the walls of the Kingdom. It soared above the clouds to hover over Theodore, sheltering the man who wept under their comfort.

****

The people of the Kingdom ran into the new land wide-eyed with anticipation, oblivious to the sea that formed behind them. They paid no attention to the great eagle rising up from behind the walls. Their eyes did not see it fly over them. Their ears did not hear its mournful cry. They did not feel the shadow of its wings cover them.

Light dimmed, shadows thickened. Background music travelled across major keys and settled into minor ones. Songs became sounds, then only discordant noise. Colour greyed.

But the people were unaware.

Part Two: The Land of Nachash

CHAPTER 11

Abigail squealed in delight as the Duke spun her around. It was nearly morning but no one had been to bed. The Duke's ballroom was still filled with those enjoying the party he hosted to celebrate the people's new-found freedom. Abigail danced until she thought her feet would fall off. She wanted to collapse into a chair, but every time she announced she was done, the Duke coaxed her into one more dance. She couldn't say no, so she let him twirl her around the ballroom one more time.

Finally, exhausted, Abigail threw herself onto one of the couches on the perimeter of the room. "Go away, Nachash," she laughed. "Find someone new to dance with. I can't take another step."

"But I only want to dance with the belle of the ball," complained the Duke, teasingly.

Abigail tossed curls that were now in an enticing disarray and pretended to pout. "Well, I don't want you dancing with just anyone, either." She looked calculatingly around the room until she spotted a shy girl in the corner. It was obvious she was awkward and out of her league, as if she would dress herself with the very shadows if it were possible.

"Ask her to dance," Abigail indicated. "I'm sure she hasn't danced with anyone else and would love to be asked."

The Duke looked over at the girl Abigail motioned towards, and then shot Abigail a wry grin. "Yes, I'm sure the reason you want me to dance with her is because you're concerned she's not having a good time."

Abigail blushed under his knowing gaze.

"It has nothing to do with the fact that she may have the plainest face in all the land," prodded the Duke.

Giggling with very little shame, Abigail pushed Nachash in the girl's direction. Drew and Marc ambled over to her couch, distracting her from a pang of discomfort.

"I don't think I've ever eaten this much in my life," groaned Marc, flopping onto an adjacent chair, gripping his belly. He closed his eyes as if to focus all his attention on digesting the enormous feast he'd consumed.

Drew shook his head and laughed at Marc. "You

didn't need to try everything tonight, you know. I'm sure there will be other opportunities to taste the delicacies of the Land of Nachash." Drew prodded Marc with his foot. "Are you joining the wrestling contest that's being held at first light?"

Marc opened one eye, lazily. "I don't think I'll be moving until sometime next week. I'll leave this match to you." Closing his eyes again, he questioned Abigail. "So, is living with the Duke everything you imagined it would be?"

Abigail's faced flamed at his insinuation but she lifted her chin before answering somewhat haughtily, "Really, Marc, you don't need to be such a child about it. I'm hardly the only woman living with a man in this land."

Marc opened one eye to peek at her, then grinned. "Yes, but you are the only woman living with the Duke. Looks like our Abigail is someone important," he teased.

"Knock it off, Marc," cautioned Drew. "We've all been settling in for the last couple of weeks. Life here is different but that's why we came, isn't it?"

Marc threw up his hands in mock surrender. "It doesn't matter to me. It's just like the Duke says, 'There are no wrong choices in the Land of Nachash. There are only choices.' I was just having a bit of fun."

"What about you two?" quizzed Abigail brightly. "How do you like living in the Land of Nachash?"

"It's amazing," Drew enthused. "Life is so different

here. There might be things I miss about the garden but, to be honest, I can barely remember enough to tell you what. The Duke keeps us so busy with endless entertainment that I never have any time to think about what was. I'm totally caught up in the present moment with hardly a thought beyond it."

Marc rolled himself into a reclined sitting position to better engage in the conversation. "It's the same for me," he agreed. "There's always something going on. We're all so busy with our own lives, we barely have time for each other anymore."

"That's not allowed," Abigail said, punching Marc lightly on the shoulder. "We'll always make time for each other. Promise?"

"Friends forever, no matter what," agreed Marc.

Drew added his agreement, then muttered under his breath. "Though I can't say the same for Seth."

Abigail frowned. "What do you mean? Is something wrong with Seth?"

Drew shrugged. "Do you see him here tonight?"

Abigail looked around the room, even though she knew he wasn't there. "Parties aren't everyone's thing, but that's okay. We're all different."

Drew shook his head. "It's not just this party. Ever since we arrived, Seth's become increasingly moody. I can't get any more from him than glares and grunts these days. It's like he can barely stand the sight of us."

Marc huffed in irritation. "You know why, don't you? He blames us for forcing him to come here. All he thinks about is being back in the garden with the King."

Abigail furrowed her brow. "That doesn't make any sense at all. Why would he want to go back there? Hasn't he been listening to the Duke at all? The garden was boring compared to the Land of Nachash. And don't even get me started on the King. Whenever the Duke tells me about what I was like while I served the King, I shudder to think I could have been that simple-minded. It's embarrassing, really."

Drew nodded. "I know, but for some reason Seth is using his anger and moods to make everyone around him miserable. It's best to just leave him alone and let him snap out of it on his own."

Muted rays of sunlight began to move across the ballroom floor. Drew jumped off the chair he'd been sitting in. "Come on, you two. The wrestling match will be starting in a couple of minutes and I want you to watch me pull off the win."

Marc jested as he and Abigail followed Drew to the fight. "You're just lucky I can't fight tonight or you wouldn't have a chance."

Drew laughed. "We'll see, my friend, we'll see."

Nachash caught up with Abigail and her friends as they left the ballroom. "You can't start without me. Who do you think is going to judge the competition?"

Abigail caught his hand and smiled up at him. "Why, I thought it was going to be me," she bantered coyly.

The Duke gave her a squeeze and winked. "Decision made," he flirted back. "I'm helpless to disagree with Abigail. She'll call the winner."

"That's easy, then," she exclaimed. "If Marc isn't fighting, Drew's the winner." Abigail laughed as she grabbed Drew's hand and walked in between them.

Marc caught the jealous look Nachash shot at Drew and was suddenly glad he'd eaten himself out of the competition.

*****

Seth settled against a tree to watch the party from the shadows of the forest. The drama unfolded in silent pantomime through well-lit windows. He watched Abigail dance with the Duke in carefree abandon. He watched Marc gorge himself on rich food that spilled from overflowing tables and could almost hear the gulps as Marc chased the food down with strong drink. Seth watched Drew easily best every man in the room and saw him gloat with each new victory. And his stomach turned. What was becoming of his friends?

Simmering anger boiled over into hate. They were the reason he was here. They were the ones who'd dragged him into this land of opulent extravagance. He wanted to be able to let loose and enjoy it. Really, he did. But he couldn't. All he could do was rage against the friends who'd pulled him from his beloved garden and its King.

Seth turned his back on them all and strode through the darkness of the night. He walked until the first rays of sunlight crept over the horizon. He did not stop until he came to the edge of the sea. Wearied by the journey, Seth sat down on the wet sand. He stuck his legs out and let the pounding surf beat against his skin. Shielding his eyes against the sun which glistened off of the choppy waters, Seth focused on the thick clouds that rose like a mist from the sea.

This is where I'll stay, Seth determined.

Let the others have the Land of Nachash. He would remain by the shores of the sea, nursing his hatred until he found a way to return home.

*****

The years passed. Quickly at first. But over time they settled into slow plodding. The freshness of youth and the thrill of excitement hardened into aged experience. Memories of life in the Kingdom faded. Slowly at first, but eventually they disappeared altogether. Soon, time in the Land of

Nachash was all they knew. And time was not kind.

CHAPTER 12

Abigail hurried down the street, anxious to return home before Nachash knew she had left. Desperation had convinced her to leave for a quick taste of freedom, but having nibbled at it, she was now as anxious to return as she'd been to go in the first place.

A sharp cry for help interrupted her flight home. It increased in volume as she rushed along, so she knew she was getting closer to its source. Abigail was tempted to ignore it. If the Duke found out she had left the castle there would be a high price to pay. Stopping to help would only increase the possibility of punishment.

But when jeering taunts began to drown out the increasingly feeble cry, Abigail stopped. She glanced furtively up the dark alley that carried the cries and muttered under her breath, "I don't have time for this today."

Sidestepping mounds of garbage strewn along the path, she rushed deeper into the shadows. They twisted and contorted until her eyes caught enough light to focus. A group of burly teens were stomping on what looked like just another pile of garbage. It didn't take long for her to realize that what she'd thought was garbage was the very place the cries came from.

"Enough!" shouted Abigail, pulling at the youths in an effort to free whoever was cowering under their feet. "Can't you see he's hurt? Leave him alone!"

Rough hands shoved her aside. She stumbled and was only kept from falling by a dirt-encrusted hand grabbing at her hair. Abigail's head was pulled close to another greasy, pock-marked one.

Choking on the foul smell of his breath and her own claustrophobic fear, Abigail realized there was a very real possibility that she would be hurt in her attempt to help. The filthy teenager pressed himself against her. Abigail cried out, covering her face with her hands in a futile attempt at self-defence.

Suddenly the leering face was pushed away and Abigail fell to the street. The biggest of the boys shouted at her offender. "Look at who she is, you fool!"

The others leaned in to look more closely and gasped. Now it was they who cowered in fear. Their words tumbled over each other in hasty explanation. "We were just teaching the kid a lesson. Everyone knows you've got to be tough to survive."

Abigail ignored them, crawling over to the frail teenager. She brushed dark hair from his face and choked back tears as she saw how bruised and battered it was.

"What is wrong with all of you?" she shouted at the group. "He's much smaller than you. What do you hope to accomplish? A demonstration of your strength? Anyone can fight someone half their size." Abigail berated the young men who now watched in shamed silence.

The leader kicked at one of the rotting apples lying at his foot. "I can't see why you're so upset by all this, you living with the Duke and all."

Abigail jumped to her feet to face him. "What does that have to do with this?" she demanded angrily.

The young man looked up at her and shrugged. "He's the one that started all the fight clubs. He's the one who says we have to be ruthless to get what we want. He's the one we're all trying to be like. That's all I'm saying."

Abigail looked away and shook her head sadly. "Just go to wherever it is you stay. But mark my words, if I ever see you ganging up on anyone again, I will use my position with the Duke to put a permanent end to it!"

The vagabonds darted off through the alleys, out of sight. Abigail knelt back down beside the young man who still lay crumpled on the stones. "Are you going to be ok?" she whispered.

He opened his eyes to look at her and attempted a weak smile. "I'll survive. It sure hurts though."

Abigail nodded. "I can see that it would. Do you have anywhere to go? Is there anyone who takes care of you?"

The young man shook his head and said simply, "My Father is away."

"You don't look old enough to be on your own," scolded Abigail gently.

He shrugged noncommittally before smiling at her. "Maybe I could come home with you?"

Abigail warmed at the look in his eye. How long had it been since someone had liked her just for her? Other than Drew and Marc, she really didn't have any friends. Sure, all the women in the land wanted to be like her. They dressed like she did. They tried to style their hair like hers. But none of them cared about anything other than trying to get closer to the Duke. They all wanted to elevate their own status.

A feeling of tenderness came over her. "I wish I could take you home, too," she murmured. She had begged. She had pleaded. She had bargained. But the Duke would not allow her to have children. He was adamant that her body not be ruined by the effects of motherhood.

Looking at the young man, she couldn't help but let the dream breathe a little. "What's your name?" she asked softly.

"Joshua." His voice was gentle but it didn't lack strength.

"Joshua, that suits you perfectly," remarked Abigail. In that moment she knew she couldn't leave him to his own devices on the street. "Maybe you can stay with me for a little while. It would have to be a secret, though. Nachash would be furious if he found you." She worried aloud at the thought, "How is this going to work?"

Joshua answered earnestly, "I am very good at hiding and staying out of sight. I don't need to eat very much at all. I won't be a bother."

Abigail took his dirty face in her hands. "We will make this work, you and I," she promised. "You just have to trust me and do exactly as I say."

Joshua nodded solemnly.

Abigail grabbed his arm. "Time's wasting. We need to hurry to make it home before the Duke arrives."

They half-walked, half-ran down the street. Abigail's mind turned as quickly as her feet. It had been months since she'd been allowed to go anywhere on her own. If the Duke wasn't with her, one of his guards was always at her side. This morning, when Nachash had left early for a meeting and had taken his personal guards with him, she'd risked slipping out of the castle for a breath of fresh air. Alone.

The Duke didn't trust her. There had been a time when he had trusted her adoration of him, but time's relentless march had cut a wide swath of distance between them. Somewhere through the years, passion had turned to possession and love had become control. Abigail had slowly begun to see the Duke for who he really was. It had always been more about power than love. Glancing at Joshua, who walked unquestioningly beside her, she tried to remember when everything had changed.

CHAPTER 13

Abigail quietly pushed the front door open. She listened cautiously until she was satisfied with the silence. She motioned to Joshua to steal in behind her. They crept through the foyer towards the staircase and ascended on tiptoe. Suddenly a door burst open below them and angry voices chased them up the stairs. The Duke was home and he wasn't happy.

Frantic to get Joshua hidden safely, she steered him into her room. Slipping in behind him, Abigail softly pushed the door closed behind her. Motioning to her wardrobe, she indicated for him to crawl inside. "Quickly, Joshua," she whispered. "The Duke is close behind us!"

He nimbly folded his body into the dark space and

smiled at her before melting into the shadows.

"Don't come out, no matter what you hear," Abigail instructed as she closed the wardrobe. "He hasn't seen you and won't think to look for you. Just, please, don't make any noise, and stay there until I tell you otherwise."

Abigail took his silence as acquiescence and hurried to sit at her dressing table. She fiddled with her hair in a desperate attempt to calm her trembling fingers. She tried to breathe deep and still her racing heart, but when Nachash burst into the room shouting angrily, Abigail dropped the brush, unable to hide her fear. "Nachash," she breathed. "You startled me."

The Duke stood over her menacingly. "Did I, my dear?" he snarled sarcastically. "I thought I'd been clear about you not leaving without an escort, Abigail."

Abigail stood to her feet, attempting to erase some of the height difference. "There's nothing to be upset about, Nachash. I had only planned to stroll through the gardens when I remembered about my new dress. I've been waiting for it for so long that I thought I'd quickly run into town to see if the seamstress was finished with it. I didn't think you'd want to be bothered with insignificant details like that, you being so busy running this land." Abigail lied easily, hoping her attempts at flattery would cool the Duke's rage.

Nachash grabbed her arm roughly, jerking her closer.

"I decide what details I bother with, not you. So where is this new dress you so desperately had to see?" he demanded.

Abigail feigned irritation. "The seamstress still isn't done with it," she complained. "I may have to hire someone new to do my work. I don't know how much longer I can stand her incompetence."

The Duke sneered at her. "Indeed. I will make sure your seamstress is punished adequately for this oversight."

Sickened by the consequences of her lie, Abigail tried to change his mind. "Nachash, give her one more chance. Really, when you consider all the lovely work she's done for me in the past, I don't think it's too much to ask."

Nachash laughed off the suggestion. "You forget I am not a man of second chances."

Abigail trembled in fear. The Duke's hand came out so quickly she had no time to react. His slap set her head spinning. She felt blood trickle down her split lip, and cowered as he grabbed her hair, pulling her against him.

"Consider yourself warned," he snarled, pushing her back into her chair. The Duke strode from her room, slamming the door behind him.

Abigail wearily rose to her feet, pressing her hand against her burning cheek. Turning to her bed, she lay down and buried herself in her pillow. The pain of her bruise didn't run nearly as deep as the pain in her heart. She didn't hear the wardrobe door open or Joshua's footsteps tiptoe closer. But she felt his gentle hand stroke back her hair. Abigail knew she should send him back to the safety of the wardrobe, but she kept him close instead.

Tears ran down his dirty cheeks and mingled with hers, staining the pristine white of her bedding while they cried.

CHAPTER 14

Abigail startled awake, trying to clear away the confusion of sleep. Her eyes pulled into focus and she saw that she'd slept with her head cradled in Joshua's lap. He still dozed and she stared at him in wonder. He brought out an emotion she couldn't name, but one that seemed somehow familiar.

Gently she whispered his name. "Joshua, wake up."

Abigail held a hand over his mouth as his eyes popped open, afraid he wouldn't remember where he was and would cry out in fear. When she was sure he'd stay quiet, she pulled her hand away. "You need to sneak back into the wardrobe. The Duke could return at any moment. This isn't safe."

Joshua stroked her bruised cheek gently, his eyes filled with sadness. He looked at her with wisdom that defied his years. "All will be well again someday, Abigail," he murmured.

Abigail gave his hand a quick squeeze before sending him to his hiding spot. She sat down in front of her mirror, attempting to fix the mess of her hair and face. Satisfied she was presentable if not beautiful, she cracked open her door and snuck down the staircase.

The sounds of Drew and Nachash arguing floated up the staircase from behind a closed door. Curious to hear what they were fighting about, she tiptoed over to the door, pressing against it to listen.

"You demean both me and my position with your ideas," shouted Drew angrily.

Nachash snarled menacingly. "Don't forget your position, Drew. You work for me; you fight for me!"

"Yet you threaten my very life with a fight to the death?" demanded Drew. "It's insanity! You're turning the people against each other and it isn't right!"

"Right?" laughed Nachash cruelly. "What is that and who decides?"

Leaning in tight against the door, Abigail started in alarm when something crashed against the wall near her head. Heavy feet stomped closer and Drew shouted, "Mark my words, you're making a mistake! This time you've gone too far!"

Abigail tried to shrink, unseen, into the corner of the hallway as the door flew open. Drew stormed from the room, but the Duke's words pulled him to an abrupt stop. Drew stood framed in the doorway with his back to the Duke as Nachash mocked cruelly. "Don't tell me the mighty Drew is worried about losing not just his position but potentially his very life? You pretend to be fearless, but I can smell it all over you."

Drew tossed his head in disgust and slammed the door shut without bothering to answer the Duke. Abigail tried to stay hidden as Drew stomped into the hallway, but Drew wasn't the Chief of the Guards for nothing. Always aware of his surroundings, his sharp eyes quickly caught Abigail crouching in the corner. He walked towards her and immediately took in the bruise she'd tried so hard to hide. Drew shook his head in pity.

"Abigail, you know why Marc and I stay employed with the Duke, don't you?" he whispered urgently.

She shook her head nervously, motioning him to leave.

"We stay to keep an eye on you. Just say the word and we'll take you out of here," Drew continued, ignoring her pleas for silence.

Hearing the Duke's footsteps, Abigail began to tremble. Drew pointed out the window to the pathway that wound through the garden. Motioning for her to meet him at their secret spot, he turned and left the castle.

Abigail remained frozen in place when she heard the Duke kick a chair and swear loudly. His footsteps pounded towards the open door and she didn't even dare to breathe until she saw Nachash storm out of the castle. When she was sure he was gone, she crept back up the stairs to her room. She would wait to join Drew in the garden. She had to be sure Nachash wouldn't interrupt their clandestine meeting.

Abigail waited for what felt like hours. Finally she heard Nachash gallop down the street on his horse. She gathered up frayed threads of courage to leave her room for the garden. Abigail settled on a bench that was nestled under a mess of thick branches. She analyzed the unruly growth and wondered why its unkempt appearance always surprised her. What made her expect something different? What pulled at her memory and made her think this garden could look different?

Drew and Marc emerged from the shadows, pushing back her thoughts. They sat down on either side of her, each taking a hand. "Has he ever hit you before?" questioned Drew gravely.

Abigail shook her head. "Never. There have been

times I thought he would, but he's never actually laid a hand on me before today. He's changing."

Marc stroked her hand in comfort. "I wonder if he's always been this way. I wonder if it's we who are changing."

Abigail looked at Marc in surprise. "What do you mean? Are things not as they have always been?"

Marc shook his head. "No. Nachash has worked hard to make us believe that this land is all there is, and that its all that ever has been or will be." Marc waved his hand at their surroundings. "Most of the people don't remember anything except for the Land of Nachash. And most are happy to keep it that way. But, Abigail, rumours are swirling. Things are changing and some of the people are beginning to remember."

Drew shook his head at Marc, motioning for him to keep quiet. Abigail noticed and immediately became defensive. "If you know something, tell me. We can trust each other, can't we?" she finished, vulnerability saturating her words.

Drew looked down at his feet before speaking. "Do you remember a man named Theodore?"

Something inside Abigail responded to the name as if it was familiar, but she couldn't think why.

"It doesn't matter," Drew continued. "He is stirring up great controversy among the people. He is telling people that his mind is waking up and remembering another time and another place. It appears that Theodore can't let a thought go once it enters his head, and he believes there is something significant about the sea. He began an investigation near the edge of it, and started doing some digging around, looking for something that would make the memories stronger."

Drew leaned in close and spoke in the faintest whisper. "We heard that while he was digging in a pile of rocks near the edge of the sea, he found a series of scrolls. Marc and I haven't been able to find Theodore and speak with him ourselves, so we can neither confirm nor deny the rumours, but we've heard that these scrolls tell of a different Kingdom with another King."

"A King?!" Abigail exclaimed. "There is no ruler but Nachash! Everyone knows it is treasonous to think differently, never mind speak like this out loud!" Fear curled in Abigail's belly as she considered the implications of what she was hearing. "These are dangerous stories. Does Nachash know of them?"

Marc nodded. "We are pretty sure that he does. Haven't you noticed that he's angrier than he's ever been? More vicious?" Abigail's fingers lightly skimmed her bruised cheek as Marc continued. "It's not just you who's bearing the brunt of his wrath. The Duke is on a rampage and everyone must prove their loyalty to him or pay the price.

"Rumours say that Theodore is reading the scrolls to whomever will listen. He won't stop speaking of the King, even though the Duke threatens his very life. So Theodore goes in and out of hiding, but has managed to avoid the Duke. Nachash is furious. He won't admit to being afraid of an old man, but the scrolls speak of a young man and that is who Nachash fears. This is the one who will come from the Kingdom to liberate the people from Nachash. There are some among the people who've heard Theodore read from the scrolls who are now looking for this young man. They think he will set them free. Others are looking for him because they think he'll bring insurrection and rebellion and they want to silence him."

Abigail's blood ran cold at the mention of a young man. Her mind flew to sweet Joshua, nestled away in her wardrobe, trusting completely, loving unconditionally. She told herself that it was just a coincidence that Joshua had recently appeared in her life. She told herself he couldn't possibly be the same young man the Duke was searching for. She told herself this over and over again while Drew and Marc talked around her.

But Abigail quickly realized that telling yourself something was easier than listening to what you were actually saying. Finally, unable to listen to her friends any longer,

Abigail stood to leave. "I have to get back to my room before the Duke returns," she whispered. "Please don't do anything rash without telling me."

Drew and Marc also stood. "We'll do what we feel we need to in order to keep you safe," assured Drew.

Marc leaned in and whispered, "We have the beginnings of a plan . . ." He was swiftly cut off by Drew.

"Hush, Marc. She can't speak of what she doesn't know," Drew commanded as they blended back into the shadows.

Abigail hurried back to her room. She crept into bed, exhaustion pulling her into a troubled sleep. She didn't know that as she tossed and fought the demons of the night, Joshua crept out of the wardrobe to watch over her. She slept. She dreamed. And in her dreams, she heard the distant echo of music.

CHAPTER 15

Drew paced nervously across the castle foyer, waiting for guests to arrive. It was the evening of the big fight and much was at stake. There wasn't a man in the Kingdom who wasn't willing to watch the spectacle of a fight to the death. Any man in the land had permission to challenge Drew to a fight to vie for his position of Chief of the Duke's personal guards. Drew was confident in his chances, but his nervousness wouldn't go away completely.

"You look eager to start," grinned Nachash as he watched Drew pace. "I can't wait to see what the men think when they see the rules." Nachash began to laugh uproariously. "Tonight the only rule is, there are no rules. A fight to the finish and the last man standing wins!"

Drew looked away from the Duke and shuddered. Some of the people said they were beginning to remember life in another Kingdom, but he couldn't even remember back to the way things had been when they first entered the Land of Nachash long ago, never mind another Kingdom.

Whatever distant memories he'd had of contagious excitement, the fun of new-found freedom, admiration, awe . . . they'd long been buried. Drew tried to remember a time he'd looked at the Duke in admiration, but the only emotion he could drum up now was disdain.

He tried to hide his revulsion at the Duke's expression. The Duke was loyal to no one but himself and cared about no one but himself. Drew felt his rage build. He'd show the Duke what he was capable of. After tonight there would be no doubt who the champion was.

****

Thomas sat in the corner of the room watching Drew fight. His stomach twisted anxiously. He was at the biggest party in the land but wasn't enjoying it like he'd thought he would. His stomach turned from eating too much of the rich food. His head swam from overindulging in the free-flowing drink. All Thomas had ever wanted was to be popular. But he'd always been one step behind.

Tonight he was in attendance at the event of the year, and the possibility of popularity and power dangled in front of him. All he had to do was survive a fight with Drew and everything he'd ever wanted would be his. It sounded so easy. He knew it would be anything but.

Nobody in the Land of Nachash could fight like Drew. And the thing about Drew, the thing that made Thomas both resent and respect him, is that Drew was never one to pick the low-hanging fruit. Drew didn't wait for the men to challenge him. Drew called up anyone in attendance who he thought was itching for a fight. He purposely picked the men who'd give him the best fight. And while the night was young, it already seemed clear that no one would be able to defeat him.

Thomas had watched Drew make sport of losers in other fights. But before tonight, he'd never seen Drew finish them off. He'd never watched life seep out and run away in rivers of blood and he'd never looked into sightless eyes.

Thomas knew that nothing about tonight was a fair fight and almost everything about the evening made him want to escape. But still, Thomas stayed. Still he jeered lesser constants along with the Duke and tossed slurs into the ring along with the crowd. Part of him wanted to avoid making eye-contact with either the Duke or with Drew, in the hope that he could evade the spotlight of unwanted attention and leave the palace alive. But the other part of him flirted with the chance that on this horrible night, just maybe he would get what he had wished for, for so long.

In another time and another place, a night like this would have been unimaginable. But over time, the people had discovered that while serving yourself, everything else seemed to matter a little less. What seemed so wrong at first could eventually be justified.

****

Drew wiped the sweat from his eyes, searching for his next opponent. He noticed Thomas standing in the corner, cheering him on. Thomas was strong and lithe. He looked like a good fighter. Drew didn't know Thomas well, but what little he did know, he didn't like. Thomas reeked of desperation. Drew knew that was why Thomas had stayed. And he knew Thomas just might be the best competition of the night.

Nachash followed Drew's gaze and seemed to read his thoughts. "Thomas!" the Duke bellowed. "It's your turn in the ring. Get in there and see if you'll be next among my personal guard."

Drew watched Thomas shrug and saunter over with feigned nonchalance, but Drew could smell Thomas' fear as strong as cheap cologne. Too many punches had been thrown and too much blood had been spilled that night. Drew had listened to the jeers of the people and the taunts of the Duke for too long. Fury consumed him. When Thomas stepped into the ring that night, he never had a chance.

Thomas crouched in position. Drew danced around him, mocking him. He sidestepped Thomas' punches, and laughed as perspiration dripped. Drew deftly stayed just out of arm's reach until Thomas was tired. Then Drew threw his first punch. It landed hard and true. Thomas gasped as he doubled over. Grabbing his stomach while trying desperately to fill his empty lungs, Thomas left his head exposed. Drew pounced. The rage that had accumulated for years found its way out through Drew's fists. Blow after blow, Drew assaulted the helpless victim. Blood trickled from the purple swelling of Thomas' eyes. It ran from his crooked nose. It gushed from a mouth that spewed out teeth and vomit.

Still Drew fought on. With each hit he raged, "Where's a man worthy of the challenge? Why can no one even make this exciting?"

Thomas lay gasping on the floor, begging for mercy. He wept, as much in shame as in pain, as his ego lay shattered around him for all to see.

It was silence that finally penetrated the fog of rage which had enveloped Drew. He looked down at his fists that dripped with blood. Thomas' still form lay in a mangled heap at Drew's feet as awareness seeped in. Horror cooled the heat that had fueled him.

Drew heard the screams of Nachash rise above the

chaos. "Finish him off! Show him no mercy!"

Looking over the crowd, Drew caught Abigail's eyes. Tears ran down her cheeks as she sat silently beside the Duke. Reflected in the revulsion of her gaze, he saw who he'd become. Too proud to be sick in front of an audience, Drew fled. He stormed out of the ring, running through the castle to his horse, which was waiting outside. Leaping onto its back, Drew thundered into the night as darkness threatened to consume him.

CHAPTER 16

Marc had been observing the events of the evening from the back of the room. He saw Drew's frustration build. He watched rage boil over until it couldn't be stopped. And he knew. Once he'd also craved the competition. The need to succeed had been the fuel that drove him. But now the victories left him empty. Now he watched the Duke feed off their pain and it sickened him. Marc knew the Duke revelled in their humiliation, fed off their fear, and lived to incite hatred among them.

Marc slipped out the back door and headed for home. He was worried about Drew. It was obvious the time for change had come.

Sinking into bed, Marc tried to feed his need for sleep

despite the demons attempting to keep him awake.

Relieved when morning slipped over the horizon, Marc abandoned his restless tossing. Mounting his horse, Marc leaned low across its back to race across the land, following the path of the sun. Drew was known for his strength, but Marc was known for his speed. Man and beast were a magnificent sight. Both heads bowed low while straining forward, dark manes streaming behind.

Hours of hard riding brought a familiar grove of trees into sight. Marc slowed his horse from a run and guided it into the shelter of branches. Safely hidden by thick trees and shadow was a small clearing with enough space for a fire. Marc saw Drew sitting hunched over dying embers. He'd known this was where Drew would spend the night.

Drew didn't look up before questioning warily, "How'd you know where to find me?"

"I know you well enough to know that this is where you come when you've had enough of Nachash," answered Marc as he settled down beside Drew.

Drew glanced about furtively. "Be careful what you say, Marc. The trees have ears. Nobody wants their loyalty called into question."

"Forget all that!" hissed Marc angrily. "Don't you think I know how you feel? Don't you think I feel the same way?"

Drew narrowed his eyes. "You're playing a dangerous game, friend. How do I know you weren't followed by someone wanting to trap me?"

The Duke's guards were under constant surveillance and they were used to being careful about what they said, but Marc couldn't be silenced.

"We both know change is on the horizon. Why sit back and watch it happen? Why don't we go out there and make it happen?" Marc continued fervently, "We're the best Nachash has. There's no one among the people who can challenge us, but we also know it's not enough! Serving him has become repugnant. We both know there's more!"

Cautiously examining the trees and undergrowth before speaking, Drew sighed. "You think it's time for our plan."

Marc speared Drew with his intensity. "Wouldn't you say it is?"

"We haven't had time to speak to Abigail about it yet, but maybe that's for the best," Drew conceded. "When the Duke questions her about our disappearance, which he will, it'll be better for her to have no knowledge of our plans."

Marc nodded his agreement. "True. I just don't want her to think we abandoned her. She'll know we're coming back for her, right?"

Drew shrugged. "We can only hope. There's no telling

what lies the Duke will try to fill her head with."

The men huddled around the fire, unconsciously trying to keep a chill at bay. They whispered their plans, moving forward in one area before having to backtrack in another. It was hours before they could rise in resolution.

"All that's left is to find this Seth of the Sea," Marc remarked grimly. He saw Drew's face harden at the mention of Seth's name. "Why do you react that way whenever Seth's name is mentioned? You know we'll need to find him since he's the only person in the land who's an expert on the sea."

Drew gazed off distantly, silence stretching long before he finally answered. "You don't remember Seth. My own memories are unclear, but what I can't forget is how much he hates the people in general, you and I in particular."

Marc looked puzzled. "How can he hate us? I don't remember interacting with him enough to have offended him."

"You don't interact with him because, for the most part, he stays away from the people. He certainly wouldn't go anywhere near the palace. Time and distance might have dimmed our memories, but Seth has nursed his bitterness for so many years he couldn't forget us even if he wanted to, which he probably does. Seth's animosity goes back further than I can remember, but it's there. It's visceral. You'll see it when we find him."

"Why does Seth stay away from the palace and live by the sea?" questioned Marc.

"Seth works for the Duke by studying the sea and its creatures. Seth works for the Duke in practice, but in reality, they avoid each other." Drew explained.

"I can see why Seth would want to avoid the Duke, but why does the Duke avoid him?" Marc queried.

"Nachash wants to know more about the sea, but he also has a deep fear of it—he won't go anywhere near it. Seth, on the other hand, has a strong connection to those waters and he won't leave them."

Marc responded with an easy-going shrug. "I still don't know why you are so wary of Seth, but I suppose I'll see for myself soon enough."

Drew looked away for a long while before answering. "I don't remember all the details, but I do know that there is a history between Seth and I." Drew shook his head and continued. "If I remember correctly, something about him came across as self-righteous—as if he thought he was better than those of us who openly served the Duke—but I've heard rumours about him, too. It's been said that Seth has conducted terrible experiments where he's used people as live bait to attract the sea creatures he needs for his research. Sounds to me like he's no different than the rest of us."

CHAPTER 17

The sun was at its highest point of the day so Drew and Marc rode hard, hoping to shorten what was normally a good half-day's ride. They reached the edge of the great sea as the sun hung low above the waters, stretching the horizon into a band of shimmering light. They leapt off heaving horses and strode towards a strong man bent over the side of a large boat. His hair shone gold like the sun's rays; his movements were fluid like the water surrounding him. Hearing them, the lanky fellow straightened to eye their approach. He acknowledged their arrival with a short nod but said nothing.

"Seth," Drew spoke first, "it's Drew and Marc. I'm sure you remember us."

Seth's eyes narrowed and darkened as he appraised

the warriors. "I remember," he answered before muttering under his breath, "though mostly I long to forget."

"We need your help in a matter of great importance," Drew plowed on despite the cool reception. "You are the great Seth of the Sea, the only expert on the sea in the whole land."

Seth eyed them coolly without responding.

Marc, anxious to move things along, picked up the conversation. "We're looking for a way across the sea," he said earnestly.

Seth replied with thinly veiled contempt. "As the Duke's elite guards, you expect me to believe that you plan to defy his orders and attempt a sea crossing which, I'd like to remind you, has never been accomplished?"

Somewhat oblivious to Seth's hostile undercurrent, Marc nodded enthusiastically. "Yes, exactly. It's never been done before, but it's never been tried by us, either."

Seth bit off his words harshly. "You'd be the two people I'd most want to escort out to sea! I'd love to leave you there right in the middle of it to fend for yourselves!"

Drew stepped forward menacingly. "Go ahead and judge us for our positions with the Duke. Do I need to remind you that you work for him, too? You look down on us for the path we've chosen, but yours doesn't seem that different to me. We fight with fists, spears, and swords, but you use the people in your own way. We've heard about your experiments, how you use the people to further your research. Maybe our methods are distasteful to each other, but at the end of the day, we're the same. We're doing whatever it takes to serve ourselves. You've resented us for as long as anyone can remember but nobody can remember why. I'm tired of this nonsense! We can pay you well, so will you take us or not?"

Shame flickered briefly in Seth's eyes and he looked away. "Why now? After all this time, why do you defy the Duke now?"

"Do you remember Abigail?" questioned Marc.

Seth turned back quickly to face them and nodded. "Yes, what about her? Is she still living with the Duke?" His voice grew louder with intensity. "Is she okay??"

Marc and Drew exchanged a cryptic glance before Drew answered. "We've only stayed with the Duke these last few years so that we can be close enough to protect her. Nachash has become increasingly violent. The longer Abigail lives with him, the more we lose the ability to protect her."

Seth grimaced in concern. "I'd do anything for her," he breathed softly.

This, at least, they could agree on.

"Seth, it's not just Abigail. There's more happening amongst the people. There are endless rumours circulating about Theodore," Drew spoke cautiously.

Whatever openness Seth had shown when they talked about Abigail quickly slammed shut at the mention of Theodore's name. "I don't know what you're talking about," he barked.

Drew didn't buy it. "Do you mean to say that you haven't heard about Theodore finding some scrolls? You didn't know he's gone into hiding for fear of his life?"

Seth glanced over his shoulder as he shook his head. "No, I don't know anything about that." Trying to change the subject, he questioned, "Why do you need to cross the sea? If I am supposed to help, I need to know what your plan is."

Ignoring his evasiveness regarding Theodore, Drew and Marc agreed.

"We'll fill you in, but we need to go somewhere and talk where we won't be overheard," warned Drew.

Seth led them to a small hut on the edge of the beach. They followed him inside and couldn't help but stare at what they saw. The inside of the hut was as eclectic as the man who'd furnished it. One of its walls was completely taken over by an assortment of shells glued in what at first glance appeared to be a chaotic maze. Tracing his finger along a line of shells, Drew suddenly leaned in for a closer look. The shells were not placed as randomly as he'd first thought. They outlined a map, and something about the territory that these shells defined seemed strangely familiar.

Seth's voice interrupted their curiosity. "We can speak freely here," he assured them. "The Duke is terrified of the sea. Neither he nor his men have ever been this close to the waters."

The men settled down around a small table propped haphazardly against a wall and began to talk. Drew and Marc spoke of their disillusionment with the Duke, their concerns over his growing paranoia and increased violence.

"We remember a time when we enjoyed serving the Duke, a time when life seemed more innocent than it has become." Marc shrugged. "Who knew that this is where it would all lead?"

"You're unhappy with the Duke, I understand that," probed Seth. "But what does that have to do with crossing the sea?"

Drew sighed and ran his hand through his hair. "There must be something on the other side of that sea," he insisted. "The Duke is frightened by the sea and stays away from it, so there must be something on the other side. We've got to find out what it is. Maybe the sea leads us to another land, different than this one. Maybe there's a place where we can live together in safety."

Drew trailed off so Marc jumped in to finish for him. "We're going to cross the sea and find out. If we find what we think we might, we're going to go back for Abigail and will bring her to safety."

Seth eyed them for a long time. "What's the connection between this and the rumors about Theodore?"

Marc leaned in, his excitement evident. "The rumours we are hearing say that Theodore has found scrolls that talk about a land across the sea. The scrolls speak of a king. One who is powerful, but kind and loving."

Seth scoffed. "You'd believe the wanderings of an old and addled mind?"

Drew sat up immediately and grabbed Seth's arm. "Who said anything about Theodore being old, Seth?"

Seth attempted to pull his arm away, shifting uncomfortably. "No one. Maybe he's not old. I'm just saying . . ."

"You're just saying what, Seth?" insisted Drew. He narrowed his eyes at Seth. "You know more than you're letting on."

Seth slumped back in his chair. He clearly mistrusted them and didn't know if he should say more. "Okay, I have met with Theodore. I have seen the scrolls," he finally admitted.

Marc jumped to his feet. "If you know what they say, you know how to help us," he insisted enthusiastically.

Seth shook his head emphatically. "No, it's not like that. Yes, the scrolls talk about a land beyond the sea, but they don't say how to enter it. They repeatedly say to look for the way to return as if we've been there before, but they caution us to wait until the way appears. They say that the King will send his son, the Prince, to show us the way."

Marc sat down in awe. "They say we've been there?"

Seth nodded. "Most of us don't remember it, though."

"Most don't, but some do?" Drew questioned.

Seth threw up his hands in confusion. "From what I can understand, the memories come in waves. Theodore says that they start small, almost like impressions or vague recollections. Over time, they grow and become more distinct and specific." Looking down, he admitted quietly, "Sometimes I feel them. They're nothing I can put my finger on specifically, just a feeling that something I've always known to be one way, could be another, or perhaps should be another way."

Seth's voice grew so quiet they had to lean in to hear him. "Sometimes I hear the echo of a sound. I think it's called music."

CHAPTER 18

The three men planned late into the night.

"We need to make our way across the sea," asserted Drew. "If there is another land like the scrolls say, one with a benevolent king, we must find a way there so we can bring Abigail to safety."

"The scrolls that I read with Theodore do speak of that land," agreed Seth. "However, they are equally clear that we are to wait for the Prince to appear and show us the way back."

"We've waited long enough," huffed Marc. "What exactly are we supposed to wait for? The Duke's rage to consume him, the land, and all the people along with it? No! I say we make a way for ourselves."

They argued back and forth between them, but were finally able to agree on a plan. They would ready the boat the following day and attempt a sea crossing the next, as it was not wise to risk the sea at night.

With the plan in place, the three men attempted to sleep amidst images of an old man, a set of scrolls, and crashing waves.

Morning was a relief as they were able to keep busy preparing the boat for its maiden sea crossing. The men worked hard all day but spoke little. When the day drew to a close they were ready. They were anxious to leave, knowing that the longer they were away, the more danger there was to Abigail, but they had to resign themselves to one more restless night.

The sun rose reluctantly the next morning, struggling to penetrate a dense fog clinging to the waters. Seth tugged at the moorings impatiently, waiting for Drew and Marc to settle into their seats. When the two novices were finally seated, Seth released the rope, freeing the boat to head out onto the open sea. He listened to the waves lap against the wooden hull and felt the wind blowing through his hair. He tasted salt spray on his lips and felt his tension slip away. Here he was at peace.

Drew and Marc were nervous at first, but before long they began to enjoy the sensation of being buoyed by powerful waters. By the time they reached open water, they were completely relaxed. Out in the wind and the waves they were free to speak their minds, so when Seth saw his traveling companions loosen their grip on the sides of the boat, he began to voice his misgivings.

"Do you think that in light of the contents of the scrolls, it's foolish to cross on our own rather than wait for the Prince?"

Drew shook his head quickly. "Much as I hate to admit that I agree with Nachash on anything, on this issue I do. If there really is a king who is loving and kind, why would he hide away on the other side of an ocean? I don't believe there is a king, and I don't believe there is a prince coming to rescue us. I think the only way out of the Land of Nachash is to make the way ourselves."

Seth pressed deeper. "The scrolls say that we chose to leave the King. They say we don't have the ability to get back to him on our own, and that's why we're supposed to wait for the help he sends."

"I don't know if you're aware of all that's going on in the Land of Nachash since you're isolated out here by the sea, but the Duke is pretty worked up about a young man who's been spotted in the land. He's going crazy trying to find and eliminate him. I wonder if the Duke's reaction lends significance to the Prince that's spoken of in the scrolls,"

Drew admitted. He quickly continued, "But I'm not the type to wait around for some hero to ride in and save the day."

Marc snorted, "Because you're pretty sure you are that hero."

Drew rolled his eyes at Marc. "Yeah, well, you've toyed with visions of grandeur yourself. Don't be too quick to judge." Turning back to Seth, Drew continued. "What do you think? Is there a Prince coming to lead us back to the King?"

Seth shrugged non-committedly. "It's hard to say. We don't really know what or who to look for, and we don't know specifically how this Prince is supposed to help us."

"Nachash says we don't need help from a King," Marc asserted. "He says everything we need is already inside us."

Seth leaned in to confide, "Theodore and I have talked about this a bit. He says that over the years there have been many rumours of this King. He knows of people who have professed their love for the King—Theodore calls them Kingdom people—and some of these people have disappeared without a trace."

Drew leaned in curiously. "Do you think the Duke got them?"

Seth shook his head. "Theodore and I don't think so. There would have to be some evidence of that, don't you think? And the funny thing is, the Duke's men have been chasing down these people, looking for them after they've already disappeared, as if they didn't know where they were, either." Seth eyed them carefully. "You haven't heard anything about this, working as closely with the Duke as you have?"

Marc and Drew shook their heads in unison. "No! We've heard nothing about this," Marc stressed. "The Duke is very tight-lipped about anything that threatens his power."

Seth wondered if it was dangerous to talk of the King on a day like this, a day when they felt the thrill of new adventure. A day when they flirted with the possibility that they were indestructible.

Drew smiled at Seth and Marc. "Look at us," he enthused. "We're the best this land has to offer. We don't need help from a King."

Getting caught up in the emotion, Marc shouted into the ocean spray, "We don't need the help of a King trapped on the other side of the sea, or his Prince! We'll cross the sea to find a land of our own. We'll be more powerful than the Duke!"

"We'll capture the hearts of the people," breathed Drew. "They will stop listening to the Duke and they'll listen to us. The power will be ours."

Seth didn't like the gleam in their eyes. Listening to them made his stomach turn. Something wasn't right. He couldn't shake the uneasy feeling that they'd been down this path before.

"I don't know," he cautioned. "What if the power wasn't meant for us to have?"

Drew eyed Seth scornfully. "Don't tell me you're getting cold feet?"

Seth shrugged. "No. I'm here aren't I? I just keep getting the sense we are trying to grab onto something we weren't meant to hold. What if having all the power is what made the Duke the way he is?"

"Maybe the wanting does the changing as much as the having," mused Marc, closer to the truth than he imagined.

CHAPTER 19

The wind picked up as the men neared the middle of the sea. The stronger it grew, the higher the waves carried their small wooden vessel. The boat climbed laboriously to the top of a wave only to plunge down into a watery valley and begin its ascent once again. The ride was intense but instead of tasting fear, the men feasted on excitement.

"This is awesome!" yelled Drew, pumping his fist in the air.

Marc stood up, hanging onto the edge of the boat at first to steady his feet. Once he found his balance, he threw his arms into the air, surrendering to the thrill of the ride.

Seth gripped the rudder grimly. It took all of his effort and concentration to navigate the boat through increasingly hostile waters.

Occupied as they were, the men took no notice of a great bird swooping overhead, lunging and shrieking through the wind and the waves as if to warn them.

Carried away with the spirit of adventure, Marc shouted loudly. "This is the furthest from the land anyone has ever been. Look at us! We're invincible!"

Drew echoed Marc in both sentiment and enthusiasm. "We don't need the help of the King. We're the fiercest men in the land and can cross the sea ourselves!"

The words were no sooner out of Drew's mouth when Seth noticed a dark shadow slicing through the water. It cut through the waves towards their boat. He yelled for Marc to sit down, gesturing frantically at the shape in the water.

Marc sat down. Drew's eyes grew large as they darted to where Seth gestured. Marc and Drew gripped the edge of the boat as another shadow emerged, swimming towards them from the opposite direction. Sometimes moments stretch on in defiance of time. This moment of realization was, for them, one such long and terrible moment.

A school of oily beasts emerged from dark waters carried on outstretched fins. They leapt in and out of the water, racing through the waves towards the boat with lightning speed. As they neared the boat, they slowed their pace and began to circle it methodically. Then, playfully, one of the beasts slipped its fin under the boat and flicked it, sending it bouncing through the waves.

The boat spiraled across the sea as Seth tried frantically to grab hold of the boom which spun crazily from side to side. Just as his hand grasped the line, a gust of wind caught the sail. With a loud crack the mast snapped in half, almost pulling Seth over the side as it plunged into the sea.

Despite the gravity of the situation, the men clung to the illusion of escape. But their hope was only a vapour, as transparent as the mist above the waters. They were being toyed with in a game that had been fixed from the start; it was not an evenly matched competition. The black beasts beat upon the boat relentlessly with their fins, making vicious sport of it. Each new attack sent a series of ominous fissures scuttling across the wood planking at the bottom of the vessel.

"I hope you know how to swim," shouted Seth above the chaos. Drew shook his head in terror. Marc simply sat frozen with fear.

Time played its inevitable hand. With a final, neck-jarring thud, a small crevice ripped open with a shuddering groan. The boat began to split down the middle and water poured greedily into the gaping fissure.

Though the boat could only have held them a few seconds longer, it was the sea monsters who sealed their fate. With a powerful wallop of a fin, the three men and their shards of a boat went soaring through the air, landing scattered across the waters. Drew worked hard to tread water, desperate to stay afloat. It was all he could do to keep his head above the water and, despite his best efforts, he remained helplessly beyond the reach of either Seth or Marc.

Drew watched Marc, who had endured the attack in petrified silence, drift on the water for a brief moment. He was completely motionless and quickly slipped beneath the surface. Drew flailed frantically, desperate to save his friend but he got nowhere.

Seth was their only source of help. Drew shouted frantically at Seth, who was already moving towards Marc with quick, powerful strokes. He watched Seth dive under the water and held his breath in fear as Seth disappeared.

Seconds later, Seth's head broke the surface gasping for air. He twisted his head around, frantically searching for any evidence of life. Quickly his sharp eyes caught sight of a thin wisp of bubbles rising to the surface. He plunged beneath the waters again, but to Drew he looked like nothing more than an impotent jack-in-the-box.

Drew watched helplessly, battling both terror and exhaustion. He didn't know how much longer he could tread water, and the longer Seth and Marc stayed below the surface, the more pointless his efforts seemed. Drew considered surrendering to the supremacy of the waves as the seconds stretched long. His strength was running out.

Suddenly Seth surfaced. He was empty-handed but was screaming at Drew. Seth motioned towards a large piece of the broken boat which bobbed just beyond Drew's reach.

"Grab onto that debris, Drew, and hang on!" Seth shouted before diving under again. Drew saw the section of boat floating a dozen feet away but didn't have the heart to move towards it. If Marc wasn't going to make it, Drew didn't want to either.

Drew's eyes grew wide as a dark head punched through the waters followed by a tousled golden one. He watched Marc's mouth open in a gasping spray as Seth pushed him up over his head. Seeing that Seth's energy was almost spent, Drew lunged towards what could be their makeshift raft. With renewed strength, he pushed it towards his friends. Desperate to re-write what had seemed like an inevitable ending, Drew fought to close the distance between them.

Drew finally managed to shove the raft at Seth, who used the last of his energy to push Marc onto the raft. Seth hung onto the edge of it for a bit, bobbing alongside it while he struggled to catch his breath. Slowly and painfully, he pulled himself up beside Marc and then balanced their precarious salvation and motioned for Drew to climb on. Very gingerly, Drew dragged himself onto the splintered and broken remnant of their boat.

"Roll him onto his side," breathed Seth, motioning towards Marc. "He needs to get the water out."

Drew turned Marc onto his side and slapped his back viciously. Marc convulsed, moaned, then spewed the contents of his stomach back into the sea. For long minutes he alternated between retching and struggling to breathe. It seemed like forever before Marc was breathing normally.

The three men clung to their raft, happy to be out of the water but they knew they'd only survived the moment. This was only a reprieve not a stay, because the dark shadows circled closer once again. Death was a relentless adversary.

Seth raised his eyes to the expanse of sky as tears ran down his cheeks. This was not how it was supposed to end. In fact, in that moment, he knew beyond a shadow of a doubt that it wasn't supposed to end; he was not made for an end.

Seth looked at the great bird which still circled overhead. "Oh that I had your wings," Seth cried. "I would soar above all of this all. I would fly until I found rest." Marc and Drew watched the bird and, though their lips were silent, their hearts echoed Seth's cry.

The bird swooped low and cried out over the waters. Suddenly, there was a flash of light and a warm burst of wind. The men couldn't see through the brightness that surrounded them, but they were aware of a sensation of weightlessness and flight.

Seth shook his head, trying to clear the light spots that danced across his vision. His eyes slowly adjusted to the brightness but it took his head longer to make sense of what his eyes told him. Marc and Drew were seated on either side of him and the three men were being carried through the air on the back of the great bird.

Seth felt the steady pulsing of its powerful wings as it carried them over the waters, out of reach of the beasts of the sea to the safety of the shore. The bird dove low until the sand rushed up to meet them. With fluid grace, the bird arched its back and sent them soaring through the air. Seth, Drew, and Marc tumbled across the sand before coming to rest on its softness.

Silence descended. They tried to comprehend all that had happened. Slowly they sat up and brushed the sand out of their hair and off of their faces. Seth opened his mouth to speak, but before a word could pass his lips, a voice thundered across the sky. It was a voice so fearsome, the men cowered under its strength.

"Did I not say you couldn't cross the sea on your own strength? You were to wait for the one I sent. Only the Prince can take you across the sea. You have forgotten who I am."

The warriors quaked at the powerful voice. Finally Seth sobbed. "We have forgotten," Seth agreed. "Help us to remember."

This time, when the voice responded, the men almost heard a smile behind the words. "Let me tell you about a garden," answered the voice. "Let me tell you about a King and his people."

And so it was that the same men who'd long forgotten about a King now listened joyfully to his voice and the tale that he told.

The men thrilled as they remembered the delight of existing for something bigger than themselves. They ached to serve someone more beautiful than the Duke.

Water can drown, but it can also wash one clean. The water that had once covered them now dried and their strength returned.

"You are the rightful King, not Nachash," asserted Drew as the King paused in his story. "These people belong to you, not the Duke, and we will bring them back!"

"I don't think we're the men to do it," cautioned Seth. "We walked away from the King on purpose. We chose to live in this land where all talk of the King is forbidden and anyone who challenges the Duke is dismissed. What hope is there for us to return ourselves, never mind lead the people back?"

Marc jumped to his feet and strode along the beach. "O, King," he began, "we made big mistakes, but we're ready to make our wrongs right. Let us bring your people back. Let us fight Nachash! We can win, I know we can!"

"Do you forget who you belong to and who you serve so quickly?" reminded the King gently. "I made you. You are mine. I will use you to bring my people back to the Kingdom, but you can't do it without me. I have sent the Prince into the Land of Nachash. You will need his help to defeat the Duke, but defeat the Duke you will."

Seth and Drew and Marc felt their strength return and their courage ignite. They would finally face the only enemy worth fighting. Justice would be served to the very man who had deceived them into leaving the Kingdom in the first place.

Once again, they anticipated the taste of battle. Once more, the hunger for a fight coursed through their veins. This battle would be different. Their adversary was deserving of defeat. The one they championed was worthy. And their victory was assured.

CHAPTER 20

It had been over a week since Drew and Marc had disappeared. With each passing day the Duke's rages grew increasingly difficult to pacify. It was as if Drew and Marc had disappeared completely. Abigail's only comfort was knowing they hadn't fallen into the Duke's clutches; the way he raged at their absence was evidence enough of that. Nachash turned the land upside down in his quest to find them.

Abigail remembered the last conversation she had with Drew and Marc in the garden. They had been up to something; they had a plan, and she was pretty sure their absence meant they were carrying it out. Even though they had promised not to, Abigail couldn't help but worry that they'd forgotten about her.

The Duke's rages had the whole castle in an uproar. He was terrifying but, scary as he was, the chaos his presence invoked helped Abigail keep Joshua hidden. Every morning the Duke rode out and stayed away most of the day. Abigail was thankful that, for the time being at least, he seemed to have forgotten about her, giving her the freedom she desperately needed.

Joshua sat cross-legged at the edge of the wardrobe with the doors flung open. Abigail lounged on her bed as they talked. "I keep thinking Marc and Drew have found a way to escape," whispered Abigail. "What if they've found a way out of this land? What if they come back for me?" Her eyes shone with hope.

Joshua was serious as he watched her. "Why do you want to escape so badly, Abigail?"

Abigail looked at him incredulously. "Do you even have to ask the question, Joshua? We live in fear of the Duke! He's horrid and scary and yet the people do anything and everything to get his attention and rise to the top. This is a land full of egotistical maniacs who'll stop at nothing to outdo each other."

"What's the alternative?" questioned Joshua softly.

"The alternative? I don't know. What do you mean?" Abigail felt irritated by his line of questioning.

"You say that right now people live for the Duke. If

they didn't live for him, who would they live for?"

Abigail smiled. "That's easy. We'd live for ourselves. Instead of trying so hard to please someone who is impossible to please, we'd work to make ourselves happy. We'd be free to pursue exactly what we wanted."

"And then what?" Joshua persisted.

Abigail couldn't hide her annoyance. "What do you mean, 'and then what'? You're being annoying, Joshua!"

"Abigail, follow that scenario to the end," Joshua insisted. "What happens when everyone starts living for themselves? Is this a problem?"

Abigail shrugged non-committedly. "Seems like it would work to me."

"What happens when two people want the same thing; what do you do then? What if you want something but what you want will hurt someone else; who decides how to resolve this? What happens when your freedom to do what you want infringes on someone else's freedom to do what they want? Don't settle for simple solutions, Abigail. Follow it through to the end."

Abigail looked away from Joshua as she thought. "I don't know," she sighed. "People would have to come up with some way of resolving these disputes, I guess." She threw up her hands. "So maybe somebody would have to be in charge. But not someone like the Duke. It would have to be someone who could handle the responsibility without it going to their head." Abigail rolled her eyes at Joshua. "How do you know so much anyway?"

The sound of a slamming door interrupted their conversation and sent Joshua sliding quickly back into the wardrobe. Abigail pushed the doors closed and flopped back onto her bed.

The Duke's footsteps sounded on the stairs, and Abigail braced herself for his entrance. He'd left her alone the last couple of days, so the fact that he was seeking her out today made her nervous.

Nachash threw the door open and stood in the doorway, arms crossed. Abigail anxiously scooted further back on her bed.

"Where are Marc and Drew?" demanded Nachash.

"I don't know," answered Abigail with more confidence than she felt. "What makes you think I would know where they were?"

"You play me for a fool!" barked Nachash. "You don't think I know that your friendship has survived all these years?"

Abigail shifted nervously. She knew Nachash loathed her friendship with Drew and Marc. Once, when she'd still been enamoured with the Duke, she had let the men slip out of her life in order to please him. But as her disillusionment with the Duke increased, she'd been drawn back to the bond she shared with them. It felt like they'd always known each other and she trusted them implicitly. They worked hard to hide their friendship and brush it off as mere acquaintance, but Nachash had always been jealous of them.

Abigail attempted to placate the Duke as he strode angrily toward her. "They're just old friends, Nachash," she soothed. "There's nothing to be jealous about."

"Jealous?" sneered the Duke. "You over-estimate my feelings for you if you think I'm jealous." An evil gleam lit the Duke's eyes as he continued. "Do you think I made you mine because I love you?"

Tears filled Abigail's eyes. She knew the Duke didn't love her anymore, but it brought her a measure of comfort to imagine that at one time the love had been real.

Nachash plunged on, eager to hurt her. "I made you mine because it made me the envy of every man in the land. You're nothing more to me than a pretty face." Not willing to finish until he had driven the knife deep into her heart, the Duke continued. "I don't know what kind of illusions you harbour in that head of yours. Maybe you think that Marc and Drew have escaped. Maybe you even think that they'll come back for you," Nachash laughed cruelly. "They didn't get away, and they're not coming back for you. They've been spotted by the sea conspiring with Seth. They think they're escaping, and they're doing it without you, Abigail."

Nachash turned to leave. "I'm on my way out to arrest them. When I bring them back, I'll get special pleasure from having you watch their punishment." His footsteps pounded down the stairs in rhythmic accompaniment to his maniacal laughter.

Abigail crumpled onto her bed, convulsing in sobs. She'd been foolish to hold onto hope. This was all there was and all there would ever be.

CHAPTER 21

Abigail cried until she was too tired to cry anymore. Her tears had traced salty rivers down her cheeks. Now that her tears were spent, she found odd pleasure in the cracking dryness she felt as she scrunched up her cheeks, then released them. It distracted her from despair.

Abigail sat up suddenly. Why let despair win? Nachash had just told her where to find Marc and Drew. Why should she wait for them to come for her? She would go to them.

Jumping off her bed, Abigail dropped to her knees to search for a worn duffle bag she knew she'd stored underneath it. Throwing open her wardrobe doors, she began pulling out bare essentials and stuffing them haphazardly into her bag.

Joshua crawled out of the chaos that suddenly swirled around him to stand in the middle of her room and watch her. "They'll return for you," Joshua spoke with quiet confidence.

"How do you know that?" stormed Abigail. "Why would they come back for nothing more than a pretty face?"

"You're far more to them than that, Abigail. They love you. They always have."

"What is love anyway?" she hiccupped. "It is nothing more than a distant dream, an empty promise."

"Love is sacrifice. Love is constant. Love is about who you are, not what you do or how you look." Joshua continued gently, "Drew and Marc stayed at their post as long as they did because they love you like that. They wanted to protect you, and they are coming back for you."

Finished with her careless packing, Abigail sat down on the edge of the chair in front of her dressing table. She gazed at her reflection in the mirror before noticing that Joshua had moved behind her and his face was reflected above hers. There was something about his eyes. The love in them. There was something familiar in their depths that made her homesick. For what, she didn't know.

"I'm leaving, Joshua." She turned and took his hands in hers. "Come with me. I can't protect you here anymore, and this is our chance."

"Where would we go?"

Abigail pulled his hands in excitement. "I'm going to try to make it to the sea. I don't know if I can, but I know I can't stay here. I've got the chance to escape and I'm taking it."

Joshua gave her a long look before he agreed. "It is time to go. We'll make our way to the caves in the rocks near the sea."

Abigail had been feeling brave, but having someone who had a plan with her, made her feel safer. She knew the Duke would be headed for the sea, and traveling behind him in the same direction seemed like a better idea than being surprised by him out on the road somewhere.

"We'll get everything ready and then rest a bit. It'll be best to leave after it's dark," instructed Joshua.

The palace was quiet, so Abigail snuck downstairs and into the kitchen to grab some dry foods that she didn't think would be missed, then stashed them in her bag. There was nothing more she could do to get ready to leave so she laid down.

At first she was sure she'd be far too excited to sleep. But eventually exhaustion won over anticipation, and Abigail was lulled into a deep slumber. As she slept, she dreamed. Her dreams repeated a distant whisper.

"You are not alone."

CHAPTER 22

Abigail awoke with a start. Footsteps pounded up the stairway. The Duke had returned and it sounded like there were many men with him. Why was he back? Where was the quiet she needed to escape? The evening was young enough that much could still go wrong and derail her plans before she'd had a chance to enact them.

Dread rolled in Abigail's stomach like a bad meal when she heard the footsteps stop outside her door. For once, Nachash didn't push the door open but stayed on the other side and knocked. Abigail opened the door carefully, fearful Nachash would see the plan written all over her face.

"Nachash," she breathed. "What a surprise! What would you like?" She prayed her voice wouldn't betray her.

"I'm entertaining some of the guard tonight and I expect you downstairs in half an hour. You'll be performing for us so make sure you look your best," commanded Nachash before turning and leaving abruptly.

Abigail's heart sank. She had to sing tonight? She hadn't sung for the Duke in ages. Music frustrated her and she avoided it at all costs. Though once she had enjoyed it, now it seemed to consist of nothing more than jarring sounds and discordant braying. It left her feeling lost, like something of great value danced beyond her grasp.

She locked the door behind Nachash and hurried around her room, focusing on what she knew she did well. Nachash expected her to look her best, and that she could do with very little thought. Abigail reached for the dress she knew was his favourite, then arranged her blond curls in front of the mirror.

She analyzed her reflection critically. Her flushed cheeks could just look like excitement over the performance, she reasoned. This would please the Duke.

Taking a deep breath to steady her hand, Abigail began applying her makeup. She leaned in as she brushed colour on her cheeks and eyes, and pursed her lips to artificially brighten them, too.

Finishing quickly, she sat looking at her reflection in the mirror. Even she knew she had a pretty face. Was there anything beyond its surface, she wondered? With the exception of Joshua, when was the last time she'd thought of someone other than herself? When was the last time she'd put anyone else's needs ahead of her own?

Abigail knew she needed to reign in her thoughts and gather her courage. She noticed Joshua sitting cross-legged in the open wardrobe, watching her closely. She shrugged at him as if to say it's now or never.

"You'll sing for him?" he questioned.

"What choice do I have? You heard his command." Feeling overwhelmed, she choked back tears and admitted, "How can I sing tonight? What will I sing?"

Joshua stared at her intently. "Abigail, can you remember singing for anyone other than the Duke?"

"Obviously. I think everybody in the land has heard me sing," she snapped irritably.

"Is there anyone else you remember?" he probed.

Abigail shook her head. "What else is there to remember? This is all there is."

"Sit back down and close your eyes," he instructed.

Abigail sat obediently with eyes closed.

Joshua began to speak softly, "Once upon a time, there was a garden of great beauty and melody. Colours danced in the music. Light sang away the darkness. Love's harmony banished fear. This garden was ruled by a King who loved his people deeply. They were his greatest joy and delight. In the midst of the garden danced a beautiful girl who sang from her heart to this King. The sound was like water bubbling over the rocks, birds chirping in carefree abandon, wind caressing the branches. The sound was music."

Abigail let the story carry her away to a mythical place. She felt a gentle tugging begin in her heart. The story seemed familiar, somehow. Her eyes flew open.

"Joshua, why do you speak of a place such as that?" she demanded.

Joshua smiled at her. "Wouldn't you long for that kind of place?"

"Oh, yes," she breathed. "That's what I imagine lies beyond the sea. That's where I imagine I could escape to."

Joshua stepped out of the wardrobe and came to clasp her hand between his. "What if I told you this place was real? What if this is the land you came from?"

Abigail gasped and pulled her hand away. "Joshua, don't talk like that! It's dangerous to even consider anything other than what is. It plants false hope and could get you killed if the Duke hears it."

"Abigail," implored Joshua, "what if it is more dangerous to think that *this* is all there is? What if this is false and what is true lies just beyond what you can see?"

Abigail felt something stirring within her as the

pulling intensified. "I need to go. I don't want to keep the Duke waiting. Thank you for trying to cheer me up!" She gave him a quick kiss on the cheek before slipping through the open door, trying not to let the look of sadness that stole over his face unsettle her as she rushed away.

The Duke met her at the foot of the stairs and kissed her cheek possessively. "You look lovely, my dear," he smiled at her, but she knew they were only empty words spoken for the benefit of the men gathered in the next room.

The Duke escorted Abigail to the front of the room. She waited as the men settled into their chairs for the performance. She avoided the gaze of the Duke, intimidated by the threat in his eyes. Closing her eyes, she tried to find the music. All she found was silence.

Desperate, she let her mind wander to the garden that Joshua had just described. She pictured the peace and the beauty. She pictured the King. The music began slowly and Abigail released herself to the notes building inside her that only she could hear. At first, the music swirled through minor keys. Abigail freed the notes on their haunting journey. The tempo increased and she raised her head to let the music soar from the depths of her being. Mournful notes of longing merged with majestic majors. It began a song of hope. Abigail threw her arms upwards as she finished in a powerful crescendo.

The song ended and she bowed her head once more, unable to look at the Duke. What if he read her heart in the music? What if he knew she sang not for him but for the possibility of another?

"Bravo! Beautiful as always!" The Duke swept Abigail off her feet and into his arms in an elaborate show. "I have enjoyed the best the land has to offer. You are the perfect match for me."

Abigail breathed a sigh of relief. Nachash remained deaf to her inner longings. As soon as she was sure she wouldn't arouse suspicion, she excused herself and returned to her room. Retreating to its relative safety, Abigail closed the door firmly behind her. She leaned back against it. It was done.

She peeked into the wardrobe and saw Joshua sleeping soundly. Quietly closing the door, she curled up on her bed, longing for a few hours of sleep before they left. As she drifted into sleep, a voice spoke into the silence,

"I've missed you, my daughter."

Abigail sat bolt upright in bed. Joshua slept. The Duke was downstairs with his comrades. She was alone. "Who spoke?" whispered Abigail.

The voice spoke again, gentle but strong. "It is I. The King. Get some sleep, my dear. We will meet again soon."

Abigail lay back, heart racing. How was she supposed

to go to sleep? She'd just heard the voice of a king! Which king, her mind wondered? What kind of king would speak like that to her? Why did he say they would meet *again*? Why did her heart respond like it did to his voice?

Questions tumbled over each other in her mind. Though sleep seemed like an impossibility, it eventually claimed her by enticing her with dreams of a place she could call home.

CHAPTER 23

Seth, Drew, and Marc hurried to Theodore's house, planning out loud as they journeyed. "We'll get the scrolls from Theodore." Seth assured them as he continued, "He'll give them to us once he's heard our story. Between our experience and what's written in the scrolls, he, and the rest of the people, will listen and believe us."

The voice of the King spoke before Drew or Marc could answer. "I have been whispering to the people ever since you left the Kingdom; most don't hear. The time has come for me to shout loudly."

Drew grinned up at the sky. "Kind of like you had to

do with us?"

"Yes, Drew, it will be something like that," answered the King. "In three days' time I'll send a great and powerful storm to show myself to the people."

Marc rode behind the others and remarked to himself quietly, "Am I the only one terrified of this storm?"

"Don't be afraid, Marc. The storm will only affect those who won't listen. I promise not to leave you," assured the King. "Your job is to warn the people that the storm is coming and that the only safe place to hide is in the caves of the rocks near the sea. You do your job and leave the results to me."

****

A loud pounding at the door pulled Theodore cautiously from his chair. His heart beat fast. Unannounced visitors were rarely a good thing. What if today was the day the Duke came for him? He limped to the door, but not until he'd made sure the scrolls were safely hidden from sight. If anything happened to him, there were people who would know where to find them. The scrolls must be preserved. It was how the people would hear of the King.

Feeling the ache of his age, Theodore slowly cracked open the door to see three disheveled men peering anxiously through the crack. His face lit upon recognizing Seth, but switched to guarded caution when he realized Seth was accompanied by Drew and Marc. Everyone in the land recognized the Duke's henchmen, and Theodore was in no position to trust them.

Propelled by the urgency of their situation, Seth rushed the wizened old man, pushing his way gently through the door rather than waiting respectfully for him to invite them in. "Theodore, let us in quickly. Please trust me. They're okay," he said, gesturing towards Marc and Drew. "We've heard the voice of the King!"

Theodore clutched at Seth as his face broke out into a wide smile. "He hasn't forgotten us? His promises are true?" breathed Theodore. Wiping away tears, he looked deep into Seth's eyes. "You search for knowledge and the truth. Have you found it, Seth?"

Seth was surprised by the emotion that surged through him. "I have indeed, Theodore! Nothing will ever be the same again!"

Theodore pulled Seth into an embrace, and then led the men into his kitchen. They sat around the table and took turns telling Theodore all that had happened. They felt freedom in his presence and spilled out the whole of their stories, holding nothing back. Theodore sat at the edge of his seat as they recounted the attack of the massive creatures of the sea during their attempt to cross. He gasped as they described their rescue by the great bird. When they shared the words of the King, tears poured unashamedly down his wrinkled cheeks.

"He hasn't forgotten us! I knew it to be true! But it's so hard to really know something your eyes can't see and your ears haven't heard. Do you think I will hear his voice?! Oh, the thought of it fills my heart with joy," whispered Theodore reverently.

Theodore spoke in an excited jumble of words as he jumped up from the table to begin preparations. "Do you men understand what all this means? The time has come for the Prince, the one whom the King spoke to us about! He will lead us back to the Kingdom. Our return is imminent!" Theodore's eyes burned with intensity. "The King is right—we must warn the people. They must be told to run to safety in the rocks. Perhaps there the Prince will show himself."

CHAPTER 24

Drew led the group cautiously through the Land of Nachash while Marc rode at the back. They kept alert for any sign of the Duke or his guards. Theodore stayed beside Seth in the middle. Though they were on a mission from the King, they were still careful to stay hidden among groves of trees as much as possible.

"If we get arrested, we'll never get the warning out to the people," Drew spoke grimly.

Marc nodded anxiously. "By now the Duke will have all his guards out looking for us. We'll get no mercy from him. You know how he feels about being betrayed."

Seth remained calm. "We can trust the King," he spoke confidently. "If He's sent us on this mission, we can trust he'll help us see it through."

"I believe the time has come for the Prince to lead us home," spoke Theodore in excitement. "The more we read the scrolls and talk of the King, the more I remember of him and the Kingdom." Theodore patted the bag he'd tied around his waist, which contained the scrolls. "I can now remember the day we left. The King wept." He wiped away tears as he remembered. "He promised not to leave us alone."

Theodore pointed up to the great bird flying above them. "There's something familiar about that bird," he quipped. "Have you noticed how it stays above us and how we ride under the shadow of its wings?"

The men glanced up. "It's the same bird that saved us when we were out on the sea," said Marc.

"Yes, I gathered that," answered Theodore, "but there's something about it that makes me think I've seen it before."

As the men rode and watched the bird flying above them, they began to recall bits and pieces of life in the Kingdom. The more they remembered, the more memories began to surface and they thrilled at sharing them with each other.

They came to the edge of a thick stand of trees and

looked ahead. Before them lay the largest village in the land. It was time to leave the cover of secrecy and ride out into the open. They looked at each other without saying anything; no words were needed. The time had come to put what they'd experienced into action.

Nudging their horses on, they rode into the centre of town. They called out loudly to the people, "Assemble in the town square! We have a message to share!"

As they rode through the streets, people streamed behind them, following them almost unquestioningly to the town square. The people were curious to see the Duke's greatest warriors accompanied by two strangers. Drew and Marc had been gone long enough for rumours to have run riot. The fact that they'd disappeared the night after the fight was decidedly suspicious. The people were intrigued to see men who they knew were living on borrowed time riding around in the open.

When quiet had settled over the people, Theodore spoke. His voice carried with strength and conviction. But instead of speaking his own words, Theodore read from the scrolls. He told the people of the King.

When he was finished, he rolled the scrolls back up and returned them to his pouch. "This is no simple story," he told the people. "The King that I have spoken of to you, is real. His Kingdom exists and is just over the distant waters. That

Kingdom was our home before we came to live in the Land of Nachash, and the King is calling us to return. Who will come?"

The people immediately began to contradict what they'd heard.

"You expect us to listen to mutinous words of a king in the presence of the Duke's fiercest warriors?" they laughed.

Drew and Marc spoke loudly over the babble. "Your doubt doesn't surprise us. It once filled us, as well. That is, until we tried to cross the sea to reach the Kingdom ourselves."

The people's eyes bulged as Drew and Marc recounted their attempt to cross the sea. They stared incredulously when the men told them that they'd heard the voice of the King.

Drew warned the people gravely, "We've heard the King speak. He will make his presence known with a great and terrible storm in two days' time. The only safe place will be the caves in the rocks by the sea." Drew gestured to his friends. "We believe that after the storm has passed, the Prince will make himself known and will show us the way back to the Kingdom. So pack what little you need and join us by the sea!"

Having heard all the men had spoken about, some of the people responded with relief and joy. They hurried from the square with jubilant purpose to pack their belongings and head for the caves. But to the surprise of the men, many of the people mocked their warning.

"You are under the influence of strong drink," shouted one of the people.

"You're here under the orders of the Duke to flush out the traitors among us," accused another.

Theodore watched the people argue amongst themselves while the great bird flew above, calling out to them. Suddenly Theodore remembered. "The eagle!" he shouted, pointing skyward. "That is the Kingdom Eagle! Do you remember how it flew before the King, announcing his presence?" Theodore sputtered in his excitement.

"He's right!" shouted Seth above the commotion of the people. "It's the same bird that warned us before we attempted to cross the sea. It carried us safely to shore even though we didn't listen to its warning. It's been the King leading us all along!"

"Listen!" Drew shouted. The people quieted quickly at the command of the mighty guard of Nachash. "We have to leave and warn the other villages, but that is the King's bird. Keep your eyes on it; it will lead you to safety."

Drew turned to Marc, Seth, and Theodore. "We must leave this village. We've warned them and told them the way of escape. What they do with this knowledge is now up to them. We need to visit all the villages before time runs out."

The men nodded their agreement and set off for the next village to repeat their warning. As they went from place to place, the response was always the same. There were those who listened and immediately took action. There were also those who listened quietly and with conviction, but in the end, allowed others to convince them to do nothing. And then there were others who listened, but heard nothing and mocked them openly.

CHAPTER 25

The day of the impending storm dawned bright and clear. Seth, Drew, Marc, and Theodore were consumed with intensity. The people had all been warned but there were many who did not listen. Desperation made the men decide to separate so they could ride into each village with one final word of warning.

"Run to the caves in the rocks! Run for safety!" They shouted until they were hoarse.

Theodore, Seth, Drew, and Marc met at the gaping entrance into the great rock caves, completely exhausted. The eagle dove and plunged, swooping through the air between the villages and the rock. Crowds of people followed the bird, running towards the safety of the rock. Others ran amongst those who were attempting to escape, laughing and ridiculing them, trying to block their way.

"The sun is shining! It's a beautiful day that is no different than any other, and you warn us of a storm?" they mocked.

"You, who are warriors of Nachash, want us to run to the rocks? Ridiculous! This is a trap," called out others.

"The Duke rides in this direction as we speak. Just wait until he arrives. Then you will know fear!" warned even more.

Though they feared the Duke and believed his arrival to be imminent, the men were undaunted. Marc and Drew noticed two elderly couples who, though close to the caves, were weary from hours of walking and now struggled to make it to the caves in time. Both Marc and Drew jumped off their horses, tossing the reins to Theodore.

"They don't have the strength to walk," indicated Marc. "Let them ride our horses."

Darkness can have a way of sneaking up slowly on those who are not watching for it, falling quietly before those sitting under its shadow are aware that it has overtaken them. That is how the brightness of the sun faded that day. Slowly slipping behind rapidly forming clouds, it disappeared before many knew it was leaving. The wind began to howl and rain started to fall.

Just as disturbing as nature's foreshadowing was the increasingly loud pounding of hooves signaling the arrival of the Duke. Nachash rode up through the heavy darkness followed by what appeared to be an army. Drew and Marc stood firm despite rivers of fear coursing through them.

"How dare you!" raged Nachash. "I elevated you to be my most powerful warriors. Everything in the land was yours to enjoy. How dare you betray me! And for the King?" he spat. "You are fools!" Nachash turned to his guards. "Seize these traitors!"

Without moving, the guards looked between the enraged Duke and the very men who'd once commanded them. Conflicted between their fear of the Duke and their loyalty to Drew and Marc, they stood frozen with indecision.

Drew and Marc quickly assessed the situation. Seth was the only one with a horse. There was no way they were going to be able to outrun Nachash or his guards.

Nachash did not look happy to see Seth. "I see you've found your old friend, the Man of the Sea," he blustered. "I'm surprised you'd trust someone who hates you so."

Focusing on Seth, the Duke continued, "You know they're the reason you're here, don't you? That day you left the Kingdom, you begged them to stay there with you. You cried like a baby, wanting to stay with the King." Nachash laughed cruelly at the memory.

Marc and Drew exchanged agonized looks as they began to remember. Their memories flashed with scenes from that long-ago day when Seth had warned, begged, cried, and pleaded. They had responded to him with deaf ears.

In their shame they turned to Seth. He looked at them without a trace of anger, but instead, with love.

"I made my choice to leave as much as you made yours," Seth admitted softly. "Yes, I blamed you for so many years. I hated you for ripping me from my home. But the truth is, I walked out on my own two legs and I have no one to blame for it but myself. Can you forgive me for blaming you?"

Marc and Drew nodded, too overcome to speak.

The Duke raged and berated his guards who finally shook off their trepidation to obey his orders. They tightened their circle around the trio. As the noose closed around them, Seth called out in a loud voice, "O, King, we now know you are the True King, and have all the power. We know you can save us from Nachash. But even if you don't, we still choose you."

Before Seth had finished speaking, terrible fingers of lightning pierced the clouds, striking the ground behind the Duke's army. The fearsome eagle swooped down in front of Nachash and his men, screaming in fury. Their horses reared up in fright, frothing at the mouth, before running crazed in all directions. Nachash shrieked with rage as his guards scattered into the building storm.

Seth, Drew, and Marc all stood, mouths gaping as they realized that, through no effort of their own, Nachash was no longer a threat. They quickly went back to helping the last of the stragglers reach the safety of the rock. Having brought everyone to safety, Seth and Drew joined the people huddled in the caves.

The only opening to the caves was narrow and low, but once past the tight entrance, the ceiling soared to reveal a large, surprisingly airy cavern. Branching off this main opening were many smaller caves that twisted into a delightful labyrinth begging to be explored. Fear of the sea had kept most of the people away from these caves, but the deep tributaries housed the secrets of those who had found shelter from the Duke within their protection.

Seth and Drew paused to catch their breath before taking a moment to look around at the crowd of people gathered in the cavern. Suddenly they realized Marc wasn't beside them. They frantically searched faces and called his name. Theodore heard their cries and took up the search, as well.

Seth and Drew peeked their heads out of the cave entrance, terrified at the thought that Marc had never made it inside. They watched knives of lightning slice open the black sky and cut across the ground with fingers of devouring fire. The earth shook and split as enormous balls of ice plummeted from the clouds, seeming to chase the lightning. Fire and ice decimated the land. The great bird swooped towards the entrance of the cave and came to perch on a rocky outcropping with its wings outstretched, untouched in the midst of the storm.

The people were secure inside, but where was Marc? If he didn't find shelter with them soon, it would be too late.

Theodore ran up behind them, pulling a pair of horses. He shoved the reigns into their hands and shouted, "Take the horses and go find Marc! Hurry!"

Though the scene outside the cave was terrifying, Seth and Drew didn't think twice. They guided the animals through the narrow entrance, then leapt up onto the horses' backs. They raced into the storm, struggling to see through the rain and the hail. Deep darkness was punctuated with hot light which seemed to freeze series of moments into individual tableaus.

Bruised by hail which bounced off of the ground and back at them, they nonetheless noted that they rode through the storm largely untouched. But fighting against the horses' natural instinct to return to the safety of the cave was exhausting. Nearing the end of their strength, a flash of lightning captured Marc, mid-stride, sprinting away from the caves. Catching up quickly, Drew shouted at Marc who was quick to jump up on the horse's back behind Drew.

Drew yanked on the reigns to turn his horse back toward the caves but was surprised when Marc wrestled with his hands, attempting to turn them in the opposite direction.

"Don't be crazy, Marc!" yelled Drew. "We need to get back to the safety of the caves!"

Marc pointed in the direction he'd been running. "Look! We've got to save her!"

Seth's horse pressed against theirs as he struggled to hear what they were saying over the noise of the storm. Drew and Seth looked to where Marc pointed and saw a woman and a young man fighting against the Duke.

As the woman's face turned towards the warriors, a bolt of lightning illuminated the scene. The woman was Abigail. And she was in the fight of her life.

CHAPTER 26

Abigail rode behind Joshua with an air of excitement. They had finally managed to escape the palace to make their way towards the caves by the sea.

"It seems like there are many people headed in the same direction," mused Abigail. "They seem to be in a hurry. I wonder why?"

Joshua kept the pace brisk and ignored her. Wanting to satisfy her curiosity, Abigail called out to a group of women and children racing in the same direction she and Joshua were. "Where are you going? What's the hurry?"

Joshua slowed their pace and pulled up beside the group Abigail addressed. A woman near the front of the group turned. She took one look at Abigail's face and drew back in fear.

Joshua spoke gently to the woman. "You don't need to be afraid of Abigail. She is trying to escape the Duke, too. It's okay to tell her what you know."

The woman trembled, but spoke courageously. "Two men who were former members of the Duke's guard rode into our village with a warning. They had two other men with them. One was a very old man named Theodore, the other a younger man named Seth. Theodore read aloud from a set of scrolls he carried with him which spoke about a king. Then the other men spoke and they claimed to have heard his voice."

Abigail grabbed at the woman's arm. "Which guards did you see?" she demanded.

"Drew and Marc, the men who were the Duke's head guards."

Abigail tightened her grip. "They said they'd heard the voice of the King?"

The woman nodded. "Yes. They said the King told them he was sending a display of his power to show the people the sureness of his presence. They told us the only place we'd be safe was in the caves of the rocks near the sea. The men were going from village to village to share this message."

Abigail turned to Joshua in wonder. "The King has

spoken? So he is real?"

Joshua smiled and nodded. "You'll soon see with your own eyes how very real he is. But now we need to hurry, Abigail. We've got to get to the caves just like everybody else." He instructed the group of women and children firmly before pushing his horse into a run. "Ride hard for the caves and don't stop, no matter what happens."

They raced for the caves, relieved when they saw the rocks come into sight. The sky had grown increasingly dark and thunder rumbled menacingly. Suddenly, lightning shattered the sky. Clouds swirled tumultuously before spitting out shards of ice. It was a display of nature unlike anything Abigail had ever seen. Her heart pounded as they raced through the violent storm. She clung to Joshua and kept her eyes focused on the rocks, struggling to keep her fear at bay.

Suddenly, Abigail screamed in terror as rough hands grabbed at her arm. She frantically tried to grasp onto the horse's mane, but felt herself being yanked from the horse's back and pulled onto the front of another one.

"Where do you think you are going?" roared the Duke. "You're mine! You're not going anywhere!"

Abigail was more frightened of the storm than she was of the Duke. "I've to get to the caves! Please, Nachash, we've got to escape!" she begged. Panic threatened to overwhelm her when the Duke merely tightened his grip on her and turned to gallop away from the caves, deeper into the storm.

She turned her head and saw Joshua riding hard beside them. "Joshua!" she shrieked. "Help me! Please!"

Joshua lunged towards Abigail and tried to wrest her from the Duke. Abigail hit and clawed at the Duke hysterically. As Abigail struggled, she saw a group of three men approaching through the thick darkness. She couldn't see if they were the Duke's men or not, but she knew they might be the only chance she and Joshua had of escaping from the Duke.

Twisting around so to see them better, she screamed loudly, "Help us!"

Nachash lashed out and cuffed her across the mouth to silence her. She watched Joshua pull away from the Duke to ride out of the reach of his sword.

Nachash gripped Abigail tightly and rode hard. He hadn't noticed the three men approaching quickly from behind. The crash of thunder and pounding of the hail drowned out the hammering of their horses' hooves coming closer. The Duke only experienced a fleeting second of awareness when Drew and Marc pulled up alongside him before the hilt of Marc's sword came crashing down on the Duke's head. Abigail struggled to stay astride the horse as

Nachash fell, dazed and disoriented, to the ground.

Joshua and another man rode up right behind Drew and Marc. The blond man came close and reached out to Abigail.

"Leave the Duke's horse and hop onto mine," he shouted above the noise. Seeing her hesitation, he urged her to go quickly. "We don't have a lot of time left. We need to get to the caves."

Abigail looked over at Joshua who nodded for her to hurry up. Abigail hung onto the man as he pulled her in front of him and pressed his horse into a run.

As they reached the entrance to the caves, the earth began to tremble. The man jumped off the horse, grabbed Abigail around the waist and raced her into the protective shelter of the rock. Joshua, Drew, and Marc tumbled in right behind them, and no sooner were they inside than they heard the sky remove its restraint and release its fullness.

Chests heaving, they lay sprawled in the entrance of the cave, trying to catch their breath. As soon as her pounding heart resumed a somewhat normal pace, Abigail leaned towards Drew and Marc and threw her arms around them.

"You came for me," she cried happily.

They returned her embrace. "We promised we would," assured Marc.

Drew echoed Marc's sentiment. "We'd never have left

you with the Duke!"

From the protection of their embrace Abigail looked closely at her third rescuer, who was beside Joshua. "I know your eyes," she whispered.

Seth nodded through tears. "You do."

Abigail's eyes widened as recognition slowly dawned. "You're Seth, aren't you?"

Seth nodded. "Yes, Abigail. It's me. I've missed you more than words can say."

Abigail shyly reached out to give him a hug and felt a sensation of familiarity wash over her as he wrapped his arms around her.

Smiling at Joshua, Abigail took a step away from Seth moving closer to Joshua. "I'd like you to meet my closest friends, Drew and Marc," she introduced. "And this is Seth, a friend from very long ago."

The men exchanged greetings before the cacophony of nature drew them closer to the mouth of the cave. They watched the storm without speaking to each other. An enormous tunnel of wind whirled across the land, flattening everything in its path. To their horror, some of the people who had mocked them were carried away in it. Others ran from the lightning, only to be consumed by fire that pursued them. Massive fissures opened up swallowing homes and those inside. Mouths that gaped in shrieks of terror were silenced as the ground closed back up over them.

Some of the people managed to escape but so many did not. It seemed that if the storm did not end soon, there would be nothing and no one left.

Then, as quickly as the storm started, it began to recede. The clouds emptied themselves and retreated, uncovering the sun to shine once again.

From within the shelter of the cave, Abigail and the men watched as a splash of colour began to grow and cross the sky. Confident the storm had ended, they wandered out of the cave to see more clearly. The people followed them out.

Stumbling out of the relative darkness of the cave, the people rubbed their eyes then gaped in awe as a beautiful arc of color painted the sky. The strengthening rays of the sun deepened the colour and clarity of the bow, which chased away the disappearing clouds. One end of the bow began in the Land of Nachash and the other rested in a bank of clouds beyond the sea, uniting the two lands. The people's eyes had become dull from the greyness of the Land of Nachash, so they drank in the brilliant colours they had long since forgotten.

Abigail watched the mighty eagle circle majestically in front of the coloured bow. Excitement building, she turned to her warrior friends.

"Could it be? Is this the bridge that will bring us back

to the King and his Kingdom?"

Before anyone could respond, a voice they immediately knew was the King's spoke. "This is not a bridge but a symbol. It's a sign of my love for you and a reminder of my faithfulness to you. I promised to make a way across the sea, and I will keep my promise. My son is already among you and he will lead you back."

For most of the people, this was the first time they'd heard the voice of the King since the long-ago day they'd stumbled through the garden gates. Though it had been the voice they had run from, it was now the voice they would run to. The presence of the King had been what they'd sought to escape and now it was what they most longed to experience.

It was time for the people to return.

CHAPTER 27

Theodore gazed in curious wonder at those gathered in the warm sunlight. The Prince was among them! His heart raced at the thought. What would he look like? Theodore's eyes moved from man to man, examining them closely. Surely the Prince would be the strongest, most powerful man among them, he thought. So Theodore looked at the biggest men in the cave. Were any of them the one they'd been waiting for?

Nobody stepped forward, and it didn't take long for the people to grow restless.

"What do you think we should do now?" questioned Marc, somewhat impatiently. "If the Prince is among us, why doesn't he declare himself so we can set out across the sea immediately?"

Theodore considered Marc's comment, but shook his head. "I think we've tried to do it our way one too many times, wouldn't you agree?" He pierced Marc with a glance. "Perhaps this time we should simply wait and see how things unfold."

Marc shifted uncomfortably at the reminder and nodded, albeit reluctantly. The silence continued.

"Theodore," remarked Drew, "why don't you take out the scrolls and read them to us. Maybe there's information in them that will help us identify the son of the King."

"Excellent idea, Drew," Seth chimed in excitedly. "In any case, it will be good to refresh our minds with reminders of the King."

"The people are already assembled," acknowledged Theodore. "It seems fitting that we have the first public reading of the scrolls since leaving the Kingdom."

Seth rolled some large rocks together and helped Theodore climb on top of them. Seth waited patiently with Theodore while the people dried off rocks and logs and sat down around them. Estimating that there were several hundred people gathered around, Seth couldn't help but wonder how many more had survived the storm and returned to what was left of their villages?

Seeing the people were ready and waiting, Seth

turned to Theodore. "The people are ready for you to read."

Theodore pulled out one of the scrolls and opened it reverently. In a strong voice, he began to read.

Surrounded by Seth, Drew, Marc, and Joshua, Abigail listened to Theodore's deep voice tell them of the King. He read about the joy the King experienced in his creation. He read about the King's patience and love, and also of his justice and mercy. But instead of being comforted by what she was hearing, Abigail was confused.

She raised her hand to interrupt. "Excuse me," she said.

Theodore nodded for her to continue.

"I don't really understand. We chose to leave on our own accord. If the King is just, as the scrolls say he is, how can he accept us back? We're the ones who did wrong, so won't we have to pay the price? Isn't it possible that the price we must pay is to stay in the Land of Nachash?"

The people began to murmur anxiously among themselves. What Abigail said made sense. What if she was right?

Fear had a voice. "The King wants us to return so he can punish us!" gasped an anxious young mother, clutching her child close. "It's dangerous to think we could go back!"

"You're right!" chimed in someone else. "What if going back will force us to pay a higher price than we'd pay by staying here?"

The serene quiet that had followed the storm erupted into anxious chatter as the people voiced their fear of what was still largely unknown.

Joshua stood up and spoke commandingly. "You are right in saying there is a price to be paid," he agreed.

"I knew it!" cried the young mother.

"Who is this young fool?" questioned a burly man standing close to the worried mother. "We don't need to listen to him."

"Be still!" Joshua commanded.

Abigail stared at him, surprised both by the authority of his tone and by the response of the people, who quieted immediately.

"There is a price to be paid, but I will pay it for you."

"W-who are you to speak this way?" Theodore stammered in confusion.

Joshua took the scroll from Theodore and unrolled it to a specific paragraph. Then he began to read.

Joshua read words that spoke of man who entered a garden. He was attractive and charismatic, and a desire grew in the people to be in his presence instead of in the presence of the King.

The story turned to another man. One who noticed that the more the people were in the presence of this interloper, the more they changed. The man went to the King with his questions and confusion.

"The King responded to the man's concerns by saying, Write! Write of the Prince. Write about the plan which has begun. It is beautiful, but it will not always look beautiful as it is unfolding. There will be times the plan is painful and hard to understand. You will not fully understand it while it is happening, but trust me until it is complete. Then you will look back on what has been written, and you will remember."

Theodore grabbed the scroll from Joshua's hands. He stared at the words as tears began to roll down his cheeks.

"I remember," he rasped. "I wrote those words. I wrote them while in the presence of the King!"

Joshua moved to stand beside Theodore and pulled him into his arms. "Yes, these are the words you wrote, Theodore."

Standing with an arm still around Theodore, Joshua spoke loudly so all the people could hear, "These scrolls were written by Theodore, but they speak of me."

Theodore pulled back from Joshua. "You are the Prince?" he sputtered.

"He speaks foolishness," shouted someone from the back. "Look at him! He's nothing but a teenager, and a scrawny one at that."

"You will absorb the rage of the Duke?" another

laughed. "How long will that take? Nachash will be done with you in seconds and then what? He'll turn on us!"

"Don't be so quick to trust what your eyes see. You've made that mistake before. Not everything is as it seems," declared Joshua boldly. "Were you not deceived when you left the King's garden for the Duke's land? Did anything here turn out like you thought it would? You trusted what your eyes told you then, and where has it brought you? Here! To a land that you now look for a way out of.

"I am Joshua, the one true Prince, and I have come on behalf of the King. You have become slaves to the Duke, and I am here to set you free. Tonight we will sleep in the cave, but tomorrow morning we depart. I might not look like you expected me to, but don't turn away from me. Instead come to me. Come with your questions, your doubts, your fears. Let me answer them. Get to know me. See me for who I am, and by doing that, you will see the King."

CHAPTER 28

Seth collected scraps of twigs and leaves to start a fire in the centre of the cave—one that was large enough to give off both warmth and light for all the people. As he worked, he watched Joshua move among the people. He was patient and gentle. The children in particular seemed to love him. Joshua would sit down on the floor of the cave and let them climb all over him, and he never seeming to tire of their youthful exuberance.

The adults were more cautious than the children. They'd been hardened by time, disillusioned by reality, dulled by experience. They questioned Joshua relentlessly with fear and distrust. And yet he listened to them. He answered their endless questions. He spoke of the King with knowledge and authority and love.

Marc and Drew sauntered over to join Seth. "So, we've met the Prince?"

Seth nodded. He saw that Drew was also watching Joshua closely. Drew smiled as he watched Theodore follow Joshua everywhere he went. Theodore would listen intently and then start scribbling frantically, desperate to remember every word.

"Tomorrow we follow him out of this cave and into battle," spoke Drew. "It will not be easy. The Duke will not relinquish his power without a fight."

Marc turned his eyes from Joshua to Drew and Seth. "Drew's right—nothing about what's coming will be easy. We have got to be sure." Marc leaned in and whispered hesitantly. "Are you sure?"

Seth and Drew raised their eyebrows at Marc's question, so Marc continued. "I mean, after everything we've lived through and seen, you are sure this is the one? You didn't expect him to look a little older, a little stronger, a little more like a warrior, maybe?"

Drew shrugged sheepishly. "I'm not going to lie. His looks are not inspiring."

"What did you expect him to look like? A kinder version of the Duke?" questioned Seth.

Marc didn't get a chance to answer because Joshua

and Theodore had made their way towards them and settled down on the ground beside them.

The young man and the old one leaned in to savour the warmth of the fire, before Joshua looked at each of the warriors carefully. "I'm sure you have some questions for me. Trust me, I can handle them," he smiled easily at them as he spoke.

Seth was the first to respond, but he spoke tentatively. Thoughtfully. "We've served the Duke; it left us empty. We attempted to cross the sea ourselves; we were not able. Without the Prince, we are doomed to remain in the Land of Nachash forever." He looked at Joshua closely before finishing. "We have tried the ways that seemed right to us but they failed. The time has come for us to trust what we do not fully understand. You say you are the Prince sent by the King to bring us home. I don't believe we have another option but to follow you."

Drew and Marc nodded their agreement, eyes only on Joshua. Though Seth's statement wasn't a ringing shout of endorsement for the Prince, it was real and from the heart.

Joshua regarded them carefully. "Why do you feel you need to return to the King?" he asked.

Drew stared into the fire a long moment before he spoke. "There is no true life apart from the King. When we first arrived in the Land of Nachash, we thrived on the Duke's ways. We loved that every day, every moment, centered around ourselves and our desires. We embraced the idea that we could do anything, be anything, and that everything we needed was inside of us." Drew paused, remembering the emptiness he felt after the competitions, shuddering at the pain he had caused so many of his fellow men.

"Time revealed the truth. Our reward for that lifestyle was to become consumed with greed, pride, selfishness, darkness. We are created to serve someone or something. When we serve anyone other than the King, everything becomes distorted and ugly. Only the King deserves our service, and only he can receive it and turn it into something beautiful. We've come to understand what the King meant when he said to leave the Kingdom would bring death. To stay here is certain death."

Marc sat, deep in thought. Finally, he spoke. "We are warriors. We need a cause that is worthy of our swords. If you are the Prince, the son of the King, and if the scrolls are right, you are the only one who can defeat the Duke and win the victory for the King. We'll fight for you."

Joshua laughed softly at their assessments of him and their situation, then stuck out his hand. Shaking each of their hands, he held eye contact as he spoke. "Well, then, I am pleased to have you on my side." The men exchanged surprised looks when the strength of his grip belied their assumptions based on his appearance.

A sigh from Joshua interrupted their thoughts. He stared past the fire towards the entrance of the cave. The men followed his gaze, but were too late to see a figure slip out of the cave and into the darkness.

CHAPTER 29

Abigail left the cave under the cover of darkness. She began the long journey back to her old life. If the palace was still standing and if the Duke had survived the storm, that is where she'd return. It was all that was left for someone like her. Tears spilled down her cheeks as she walked. It would have been better not to have had hope at all, than to catch a taste of it only to lose it again, she decided. It would have been easier to have been left in the darkness than to have been shown a glimmer of light and have it snatched away.

As she walked, Abigail remembered how easily Joshua had moved among the people, how quickly his laugh would ring out over the silly antics of the children, and how soft his dark eyes were, even when engaged in serious conversation with the adults.

Abigail felt betrayed by Joshua. He had entered her life in his situation of need, so she had trusted him. Now it turned out that, once again, she was the one in need, and he had exposed it.

All the way back to the palace, Abigail warred with herself. Was Joshua like the Duke? Someone who would just use her when it was convenient and discard her when her usefulness ended? Or was he really the Prince, the son of the King? Joshua knew she'd belonged to the Duke. If he was really the Prince, how could he ever accept someone like her?

The road back was rough and rocky for Abigail but she didn't stop. When the castle loomed in the distance, she pushed her feelings down and squared her shoulders for the final leg of the journey. Her choice was made.

She opened the door silently and slipped inside. Abigail ascended the stairs and walked woodenly into her room which was exactly as she'd left it. The disarray of her departure assaulted her. Open wardrobe doors mocked her with reminders of hope. She tidied up in a trance.

Sitting down at her mirror, she gazed at her reflection. She barely registered the sound of movement behind her and didn't bother to turn.

"You're back," stated the Duke.

Abigail nodded.

Nachash marched towards her and yanked her around to face him. Abigail took in the sight of his bruised and bloody appearance. She appraised the scratches across his face and neck. She had inflicted many of them. The wounds he'd given her were harder to see.

"Do what you like to me," Abigail spoke in resignation. "I'm yours."

Nachash pulled her to her feet. Putting his hands on her shoulders, he studied her intently before speaking.

"Did you think you could escape me, Abigail? You're mine. You belong to me. Did you imagine that the Prince would take you back?" He smiled cruelly as he spoke. "No, my dear. You'd never be allowed back."

Abigail felt his hand stroke her back, roughly, possessively, and she looked away. For the thousandth time she wished that she had never laid eyes on the Duke—that she could stand before the Prince without the memories of Nachash. She wished the Prince could have known her as she'd been in the garden. Innocent. Whole. She longed to breathe without feeling like she was being swallowed up by gaping emptiness.

Tears of shame and sorrow ran down Abigail's cheeks. She might be able to run away from the Duke but she could never escape herself.

Nachash held her tight that night. He whispered

plans of revenge. He anticipated the moment he would emerge victorious, defeating Joshua to block the return of the people.

Cold emptiness settled over Abigail as she listened. For fleetingly short moments in the cave, she had believed Joshua. She had believed there was a way back to the garden and that one day she could be free from the Duke.

But then, she would watch Joshua but see Nachash. She'd found herself evaluating every word, every promise Joshua made against every one the Duke had broken.

Abigail didn't begrudge the rest of the people their hope. They hadn't sold themselves to the Duke in the same way she had. They didn't share the same memories she did.

She'd managed to hang onto hope until, sitting in the cave watching the warriors and Theodore with Joshua, she'd remembered. In a flash, a scene from their past had returned to her. She was the one who'd invited Nachash into the garden in the first place. She was the one who had ultimately betrayed the King and the people.

Let the people return, she thought. For her, that dream was hollow and the wish was futile. She could never go back.

CHAPTER 30

Drew shook Seth and Marc awake. They'd dozed by the fire and it was now morning. The cave was full of activity as Joshua prepared to lead the people out.

"Wake up," urged Drew. "I've searched everywhere and can't find Abigail." Seth and Marc sat up immediately.

"What do you mean?" questioned Marc, still rubbing sleep from his eyes.

Seth was fully awake in an instant. "Surely she didn't leave the cave," he stated as he made his way towards Joshua. "Joshua, I know you're busy getting everyone organized, but we're worried about Abigail. Drew says he can't find her anywhere."

Joshua nodded, sad but calm. "Each of the people

makes their own choice and Abigail has made hers."

Drew bristled at the implication. "Are you saying she chose to leave the cave?"

"She did," Joshua answered.

"Where would she go? The only part of the land she knows well is near the Duke's castle." Drew insisted.

Joshua didn't say anything. He just held Drew's gaze.

"You can't mean she left to return to the Duke?" Drew demanded.

Joshua nodded.

"That's impossible!" Drew shouted. "She's was terrified of the Duke. There's no way, after everything that happened yesterday, that she would go back."

Seth tried to calm Drew down but couldn't hide his own fear. "Joshua, we've got to do something. Can you lead the people while we go back to rescue Abigail?"

Joshua shook his head. "No. She'll come when she's ready," he assured them. "There are some things she fears more than the Duke, right now. Give her the time she needs." Joshua walked away.

Seth, Drew, and Marc watched as Joshua assembled a small and uninspiring army. How could they leave Abigail behind?

"We don't cross the sea without her," commanded Seth. "For now, we do as Joshua says, but as we move among the people, we'll keep an eye out for her. At some point the Duke will come to fight us. If he has Abigail with him, we can rescue her then. If he doesn't, we'll sneak away from the battle to save her."

Marc and Drew nodded their agreement. Joshua was planning to lead all the people who were with him in a circle through the land. He wanted them to witness the destruction of the storm in their own villages and homes while they searched for survivors among their own neighbours. Joshua would invite everyone they found to join them. Only once this mission was complete would they return to the sea. Joshua was adamant that the King wanted all the people to be given a final chance to return to the Kingdom.

The warriors helped Joshua place the frail and elderly on horses so that they could keep up with the others. When they could see that the people were ready to set out, the warriors took their places around the perimeter of the group to keep an eye out for Nachash and his men.

Joshua gave the order, and it was time to go. The warriors obeyed, but leaving without Abigail placed a heavy burden of worry upon them.

Marc was lost in the persistent rhythm of parading feet when he suddenly became aware of a presence beside him. He turned to see Joshua matching him stride for stride. Joshua smiled when Marc nodded to acknowledge his presence.

"Do you follow me only for the adventure?" questioned Joshua.

Marc frowned. "What do you mean? You're the Prince, the son of the King. Who else would I follow? You're the only one who can defeat Nachash!"

Joshua nodded. "What if I told you that though victory was sure, the battle would be hard. Would you still follow me?" persisted Joshua.

Marc tried to hide his frustration. "Well, you alluded to that before we set out, and here I am. Doesn't it seem like the answer is yes?" Marc shook his head. "This seems like a pointless line of questioning. Why are you interrogating me like this?"

"You must choose more than just victory, my friend," responded Joshua. "You need help with more than just escaping this land. You need someone who can cure the sickness and death inside of you." Joshua's eyes were serious but his tone gentle. He didn't wait for Marc to answer. He simply smiled and picked up his pace moving on.

Marc didn't enjoy being alone with his thoughts. They led him down paths he'd just as soon avoid. Yes, he'd done a lot he wasn't proud of while serving Nachash, but he'd never been as violent as Drew. Yes, he had an intense need for action and adventure, but it wasn't hard to reason that he'd never used people to the extent Seth had. And when he compared himself to Abigail? That was easy. She'd committed the ultimate betrayal of the King.

Thoughts of Abigail pulled his eyes back to Joshua. Watching him, a niggle of doubt surfaced. Joshua was willing to leave without Abigail. This concerned Marc as much as Joshua's most recent line of questioning. Were they being naïve to trust Joshua so quickly and completely?

Though buffeted by doubts, Marc still followed Joshua from village to village. He watched how Joshua interacted with the people. Joshua was warm and gentle. He spoke about the King to anyone who would listen.

As they entered the last village, Theodore came to stand beside Seth, Drew, and Marc. "Joshua changes before our eyes," Theodore marvelled.

Seth nodded his agreement. "The more he speaks of the King, the stronger he grows."

"Yes, well, he'll need every last bit of that strength if he's to battle Nachash," Drew reminded them grimly.

Marc pointed towards the growing number of people joining the Prince. "There are many who follow the Prince now, but there are going to be many more who remain with Nachash," worried Marc. "His army will be larger than ours and he's going to find us before we reach the sea. We'll need to be ready to fight."

"We're ready," assured Seth. "There may be more people with the Duke than with the Prince, but surely the King didn't send his son out here to be defeated."

Marc looked down at his feet uncomfortably. No, they wouldn't be defeated. But still, Joshua's warning from earlier unsettled him. It wasn't going to be easy. And if Marc was completely honest with himself, that fact did not sit well with him.

CHAPTER 31

As they completed their circle through the land and neared the sea, the people's excitement grew. Among the warriors, the tension grew. The Duke was sure to show up at any moment.

They crested a hill and saw the sea spread out beneath them. The sun glistened off the water, beckoning them on. The people were eager to reach the shore. Drawn to their deliverance, they began to move more quickly.

They ran across the scarred land, churning up a cloud of dust. It obscured another ominous cloud that gathered far behind them.

Joshua moved to the front of the crowd and commanded the people to stop. Seeing a jagged rock jutting out of the ground, he climbed to the top. From this vantage point, Joshua directed the people below. "Gather on the beach at the edge of the sea. Those who are riding horses will need help dismounting. Then, those of you who are able to fight, stand near the horses and wait for my command."

Standing above the crowd, Joshua was the first to notice that the fighting men would not have long to wait. The Duke's army approached quickly, so Joshua called out to Seth, "Have the warriors form a line! The Duke is coming!"

Seth shouted final orders to those who'd indicated they could fight, then joined up with Drew and Marc in providing a final line of protection in front of Joshua.

Ominous silence fell upon all the people as they watched the Duke approach. Nachash reigned his horse to a stop and leapt from its back, headed straight for Joshua, chest heaving with rage. Quietly, but firmly, Joshua ordered his men to let Nachash through.

Drew gripped his sword as Nachash strode past. Drew's eyes didn't leave the Duke's form until the man who walked behind Nachash shoved him with the butt of his sword.

Drew swung his gaze from Nachash and locked eyes with Thomas.

"You thought you were invincible," sneered Thomas. "Let's see who wins this fight!"

Drew felt a rush of shame as Thomas rode past but he couldn't afford to be distracted. He turned his attention back to Joshua and the Duke.

Nachash stamped towards Joshua, sword raised. "How dare you assemble my people, in my land, filling their heads with your lies!" he roared.

"Your people, Nachash? If I remember correctly, you promised these people they wouldn't belong to anyone but themselves. If that's the case, they can choose who they'll listen to."

"Silence!" the Duke shrieked. "Do not speak of these things in their presence. They don't need to know the whole of the matter. The fight is between us. Leave them out of it!"

There was steel in Joshua's voice and fire in his eyes as he responded to Nachash. "Yes, the fight is between us. It always has been. The difference between you and I is that you don't care about these people. All you care about is keeping as many people from me as you can.

"But as for myself, I love them. These people were created by my Father, the King. We want to bring as many as will choose to do so back to the Kingdom with us. Before we can return, however, you and I must battle. You've wanted this fight for a long time; know that I won't back down."

Nachash bellowed, "People, don't listen to this man who claims to be from the Kingdom, offering you hollow promises of a return. He intends to enslave you behind the walls once again. He has told you that you need him and that you must serve the King alone. He lies! The Prince and the King are angry at you for leaving them and for choosing me. If you return, they will enslave you in a life of servitude in the Kingdom as punishment. I rescued you and brought you to freedom. It's with me that you're free to serve yourselves."

Joshua's voice rang out a strong and clear response. "Remember what I've told you about the King. Remember what the scrolls say about him. He is patient and merciful. He waits for you to return! You are free to choose. Stay on the beach if you want to return. But if the Duke is who you want to follow, leave the beach. My warriors and I will no longer protect you."

When he was finished speaking, Joshua looked grimly at Seth, Drew, and Marc. "It begins," he announced.

The men leapt from the rock and ran down to the beach. They quickly assembled the horses and the men who were waiting and ready to fight. The Duke momentarily retreated to higher ground while he organized his men. It was clear that there were more with him than there were with Joshua.

Seth, Drew, and Marc, along with all the fighting

men, waited for Joshua to give the signal before they charged into battle. At his cry, they ran towards the Duke, leading the battle away from the people. This would not end until the Duke was defeated, and once he was defeated, there'd be no one left to fight. Inside each of them was the distinct feeling that this would be the battle that would end all battles.

CHAPTER 32

Abigail had proven her loyalty to the Duke by willingly returning to him. He was confident that she was back to stay, so Nachash had removed his surveillance of her. But he did not leave her alone. Carried away with excitement over the upcoming battle, Nachash sought out Abigail as he tore through the palace getting ready to leave. With great relish he bragged as he readied himself.

Abigail appeared to be listening, passively if not attentively, to the Duke's boasting. She smiled hollowly as he described the victory he was sure he would win. She tried to suppress the shudders that crawled up her spine as he shared his vile plans of complete domination. But inside, her heart was pulled to Drew and Marc and Joshua and Seth. It ached at the thought that they, her friends, the men who had always treated her with love and kindness, would be defeated by Nachash.

Finally, Nachash was ready to leave. Abigail watched him ride out in front of the men who'd stayed with him. He left to carry out his despicable plan—she was left alone with her thoughts. Would Nachash really win? Could it be that evil would truly defeat the only good she knew?

Abigail wrung her hands in distress. She might have chosen to return to the Duke, but her friends didn't deserve to share her fate. Without thinking, Abigail raced to the stable. She saddled up one of the few horses that remained and set out for the sea. She knew that traveling alone was faster than moving with an army, so she was confident she would arrive at her destination before Nachash. She couldn't save herself, but maybe she could save her friends. At the very least, she could warn them. It was all that she could do.

Abigail rode up in time to see Joshua leading his people the final distance to the sea. She pulled her horse to a stop and watched him from behind the stump of a battered tree. She saw him moving among the people, spreading courage and excitement.

Then Abigail noticed Seth, Drew, and Marc, working

together as they organized people on the beach. They interacted with easy comradery and affection, strengthened by mutual respect. Loyal and protective, they were the dearest people she knew. Her heart nearly broke from longing.

"I will take you still," whispered a voice in the wind around her. Knowing who spoke, she shook her head.

"Don't give me hope. It hurts worse than the darkness," she cried.

"Daughter, faith, hope, and love can't be defeated. They will always exist. Soon your faith will become sight and your hope will be realized. Then you will see that through everything, love has endured. Love is the greatest of the three, so let my love give wings to your faith and your hope." The voice of the King urged, "Run to him, my girl!"

Abigail sobbed audibly, trying to wrestle away the longing. She dared one last look at Joshua before she determined to disappear forever, and saw that he watched her from a distance.

"Come," he mouthed, pointing towards the sea.

She looked behind her and saw a cloud of dust building in the distance. She knew Nachash would be upon them before long. Looking back at Joshua, she shook her head.

"I can't," she called out, slowly backing away.

Joshua took several steps towards her with his arms outstretched. "Come!" he repeated.

She saw the open arms, the softness in his eye, the determination of his command. Suddenly Abigail didn't know why she was fighting against him. What if he would take her back? If the alternative was a lifetime with the Duke, wasn't it at least worth a try?

Slowly the barriers Abigail had erected around her heart began to crumble. Looking behind her one more time, she turned back to Joshua and started walking towards him. Then she ran. She ran like chains had been loosed, straight for Joshua, who waited with outstretched arms.

But instead of running into his arms, Abigail fell at his feet. "Before you say you'll take me, you have to know all of it!" she sobbed.

Joshua knelt down beside her, stroking back her hair as her words tumbled out. "I was chosen by Nachash because I was the most beautiful woman in the land. He gave me everything my heart desired, and I loved it. I thrived on knowing everyone wanted to be me. Nachash chose me, but I chose him, too!"

Abigail could barely get out the words that she said next, but she knew they had to be said. "Joshua, I'm the one who invited Nachash into the garden in the first place. I'm the reason he was introduced to the people. I'm the reason we all left the garden to begin with, and the reason you're here and have to fight him." Abigail hung her head in shame.

Joshua lifted her head and looked into her eyes before speaking tenderly to her. "Abigail, do you remember what I read from the scrolls that day outside the cave? Everything that has happened was part of the plan. I know it's hard to understand, but even though you get to choose whose presence you want to live in, your choices cannot change or mess up the plan. Nothing that you've done can keep you out of the Kingdom if you choose to return."

Taking her hands into his, Joshua reassured Abigail again. "Abigail, I knew all about your life with the Duke before you said a word. But your heart has changed. Now you listen for the voice of the King and you obey."

"Nachash says that you will not want me back. He says I belong to him," whispered Abigail.

"Nachash can only have those who choose him," Joshua spoke forcefully. "You've chosen the King. There is nothing Nachash can do about that."

"Why did you leave the Kingdom, Joshua?" questioned Abigail. "You knew the truth of the Land of Nachash and you knew the truth of our hearts. How could you leave the Kingdom, knowing what it was truly like here?"

"I'm the only way of return for you and the people. If I hadn't come to show you the way back, you would have been trapped here forever. The death you've been experiencing a little bit at a time would eventually consume you. I came because both the King and I love you and want nothing more than for you to come back home."

Joshua pulled Abigail to her feet and embraced her. "Oh, Abigail, I hoped you'd see with the eyes of your heart who Nachash really is, as well as who I am. Don't be afraid. I'm stronger than Nachash. I'll protect you and bring you safely to the other side. I love you and have waited for this." Joshua held her out at arm's length and grinned. "Are you ready to see the King?"

Abigail beamed. Joshua knew all about her and he accepted her anyway. Because of him, she was going to see the King. Nothing would ever separate them again.

"Go with them" Joshua said, pointing to the group of people mingling along the edge of the sea. "The warriors will protect you and I will deal with the Duke."

"Be careful," Abigail whispered, then dashed to join the people, pushing away the fear that threatened to overtake her as soon as she left Joshua's side.

"Abigail," Joshua called. Abigail stopped running and looked back. He smiled at her. "It's okay to be scared, just don't let the fear stop you. You can trust me and you can trust the King. When you get back to the Kingdom, you will see that everything you've had to experience in this land will have been worth it!"

Joshua walked back to join the warriors who were preparing to fight. She watched him climb to the top of a large rock and saw Seth, Drew, and Marc move towards Joshua protectively. As Abigail listened to him give direction to the warriors, she felt her courage flame to life.

Renewed by her determination, she started running to catch up to the people on the beach. Finally, she knew without a doubt that the Kingdom was the world she had been made for. She didn't have any desire to look back on the land she was leaving; she only wanted to look forward to what lay ahead.

Abigail didn't see the shadow chasing her as she ran. She had no warning before a gloved hand tightened over her mouth and she felt herself being swept up onto a dark horse. Frantically, she whirled around to lock eyes with Nachash. He held her in an iron grip that silenced her screams.

"You belong to me, Abigail!" he rasped. The foul sulphur of his breath enveloped her in a cloud. Abigail writhed and twisted, fighting against the bonds that held her fast. But she was no match for the Duke.

Nachash pushed his horse behind a thick stand of trees and jumped off, dragging Abigail with him. Roughly, he shoved a gag into Abigail's mouth and bound her wrists and ankles. Once he was sure she was tied tightly, he dragged her to a thorny bush and left to rejoin his men. She was close enough to see and hear the coming battle, but too far away and too tightly bound to save her friends.

Tears blurred her eyes as she lay impotently in the dust. No one was aware of the Duke's treachery. There was no one who could help her. Though she could see the sea, which would surely become the path to the Kingdom, it was just as surely beyond her reach.

CHAPTER 33

The air was thick with the sounds of battle. Drew grunted and ducked out of the path of a heavy blade which sliced through the air where his head had been. His adrenaline surged as he struck blow after blow, leaving a trail of defeat behind him. The repetitive rhythm of duck, block, and thrust was punctuated with groans and shrieks. He fought ferociously, his blood pumping with exertion. Every opponent he struck down was replaced by another.

Drew lunged towards his next opponent, thinking to strike a death blow. He recoiled in shock when he identified his assailant. "Thomas!" he breathed. "I don't want to fight you again. Come to our side and I'll fight alongside you."

Thomas pretended not to hear and countered Drew's moves, focused in his anger. Seeing a dangerous blow coming for him, Drew reacted, slamming the hilt of his sword against the side of Thomas' head. Thomas slumped over, unconscious. A moment of regret flitted through Drew but he didn't have time to bemoan his decision. The battle raged.

He glanced to his right to see how Marc fared. Marc was fast, moving so quickly his body was a blur, cutting down foe after foe. But even though he was fast, he had his eyes trained on the battle before him and didn't see the enemy preparing an ambush from behind.

"Marc!" Drew shouted. "Behind you!"

Marc whipped around just in time to block the dagger aimed at his back. He sliced at the enemy who never saw the blade that ended his battle.

Drew ran towards Marc and pivoted so that they fought back-to-back. As a pair, they cut a wide swath through the battlefield, mowing down the enemy as the two of them moved towards Seth. When they finally reached him, they formed a triangle, fighting with their backs in and swords out.

Sweat pouring off of him, Drew panted as he pivoted away from a burly opponent. "We need a plan here!" he shouted above the din of battle.

"We need reinforcements," Seth yelled as he rolled

away from a swinging club. Unable to take his eyes off the skirmish he was engaged in, he bellowed a question at Marc. "Is the eagle still above us?"

Marc glanced up briefly. "The bird is with Joshua," he shouted. "We need to get closer to them!"

The band of warriors harnessed their adrenaline as they struggled to force their way through the thick battle to get closer to Joshua. They engaged in skirmish after skirmish as they crossed the field.

"Can anyone see Nachash?" called out Drew. "I lost sight of him earlier and haven't seen him since."

Seth grunted as a wildly howling man lunged at him, knocking him to the ground. Marc and Drew were quick to jump to Seth's aid, but struggled to fight off the man's comrades, who joined in the fight.

After long moments of hard fighting, Marc was finally able to reply. "He's not fighting Joshua and I haven't seen him either."

When they were within shouting distance, Drew yelled loudly. "Joshua!"

Joshua glanced toward them as he blocked the thrust of a spear.

"We promised to fight with you, even to the death," grunted Drew, spinning out of the reach of a vicious blow. "But you did promise us victorious passage. The battle is hard and doesn't show signs of letting up. There are more men with them than there are with us. We need help!"

The Duke's men had the advantage and pushed the battle closer to the sea and the people who were gathered along the shore. The closer the battle got, the harder it was going to be to protect them.

"We fight to return to the Kingdom, so don't worry. The King won't leave us to fight alone," roared Joshua. "He fights for us!"

"Don't take this the wrong way," panted Seth, "but unless the King sends help, we won't make it back to the Kingdom!"

"Cover me," commanded Joshua. "I need to head back to the rock for the battle to turn."

They were fighting close by the jagged outcropping Joshua had earlier instructed them from, so together they deflected the attack of the adversary while he climbed to the top of the rock.

The battle raged below as Joshua stood to his full height on the rugged ledge. He focused his gaze on the bank of clouds that obscured the opposite shore. The warriors could see Joshua's lips moving as if he were talking to the clouds.

Suddenly, Joshua thrust his sword toward the great bird which soared high overhead. In a voice that rushed like mighty waters, Joshua shouted, "For the King and his Kingdom!"

The great eagle began to cry out loudly before tossing back its head. The bird opened its mouth wide and began spewing out balls of fire. The burning orbs raced across the land, pursuing the warriors of Nachash, leaving Kingdom warriors untouched. Pandemonium erupted across the battlefield. Kingdom warriors were suddenly left without an adversary.

As the fireballs disintegrated into puffs of smoke, Joshua bellowed over the shrieks and screams. "If there is anyone left in the land who would choose the King, come now! Join the people gathered on the beach, but hurry! Your time to choose is almost past."

Groups of people who had stayed hidden from the battle, hoping to avoid it, started running out of burned-out houses and from behind bushes. They raced for the beach. Seth, Drew, and Marc joined Joshua and the warriors who fought with them to provide cover for anyone attempting to escape the Land of Nachash and head for the sea. But to their shock, there were many who, rather than running to Joshua, came out of hiding to scream curses against Joshua and the King. Some even tried to stop their fellow people from leaving.

"Stop the insanity!" pleaded Seth. "Leave your foolish

pride, stubborn ways, and certain death," he implored. Seeing his pleas were mostly ignored, Seth wiped tears from his cheeks. The number of stragglers running for the sea was small.

Seth turned to Joshua in time to see him raise his sword again. Thrusting it high towards the bird, Joshua shouted, "For the King and his Kingdom!" The eagle swooped low over the land with its beak open wide. A horde of insects marched from the depths of its throat and swarmed over the ground. They rapidly devoured the foliage that had survived the great storm. When there was nothing else to consume, they turned their ravenous appetites in a new direction. The grotesque insects began to gnaw on the people. Like the balls of fire, they pursued the warriors of Nachash, leaving the people of the Kingdom untouched.

Marc wept, sickened by the sound of masticating jaws and shrieks of agony that filled the land. He gulped great sobs of relief when the bird finally closed its mouth. When Joshua's powerful voice rang out again, Marc moaned at the thought of what fresh horror would follow.

"I warn you now, come to me for safety. Return to the Kingdom or you will be destroyed!"

Marc stood by his fellow warriors, ready to protect any who would run to Joshua or try to make their way to the beach.

He saw a man pull a woman and several young children out of a dried-up well and dash towards the beach. A group of teenagers who had sought protection under the shelter of a turned-over wagon, pushed it upright and sprinted through the battlefield for the sand at the seashore.

It took very little effort to protect those who ran for safety because many warriors had been decimated by the balls of fire or consumed by the horde of insects. There were very few of the Duke's men left to oppose their flight to safety.

Some of the Duke's warriors joined the defectors, crawling across the carnage towards the sea. But once again, others remained where they were, defiant to the end, calling down curses upon Joshua, the bird, and the King, even as the insects consumed them to their last breath.

Drew faced the battlefield looking for anyone else who sought to escape from the Land of Nachash. Had all now come? Were the rest lost? A movement near the edge of the field caught Drew's eye. A badly-disfigured man staggered towards Joshua, flailing his arms to rid himself from the painful insect jaws which clung to him.

As the man stumbled closer, Drew gasped. It was Thomas! Lurching forward with the last of his strength, Thomas crumpled to his knees before reaching Joshua. His arms reached out and Drew could hear him plead, "I need you, Prince." With failing breath, Thomas begged, "Please, give me one last chance."

Drew's shoulders shook as he watched Joshua kneel down and cradle Thomas' head in his lap. He saw Joshua whisper something into Thomas' ear, before Thomas' form grew still. Joshua stroked the hair back from Thomas' forehead as a lifeless hand fell off of Joshua's lap. Blood stopped flowing from the open wounds, and breath no longer lifted Thomas' chest.

Drew narrowed his eyes and shook his head in anger. "No!" he cried out to Joshua. "No! He came to you! He asked for mercy! Why didn't you save him?!" Drew ran to where Thomas lay and wailed. "You promised that all who came to you could cross the sea. You said that no one would be denied a return to the Kingdom, Joshua! We trusted you!"

Joshua stood up and faced Drew. "Watch," he commanded.

Drew watched Joshua kneel over Thomas' still body once again. He saw Joshua breathe into Thomas' mouth.

Thomas gasped. His eyes flew open and locked onto Joshua's. "I heard it," he whispered. "I heard the music again." Thomas rose to his feet and looked over his body. There was no evidence of the insects. No open wounds, no scabs, nothing that indicated he had faced death. Thomas stretched his arms out and flexed, then looked at Joshua in wonder. "I'm here, but all I want to do is go back there,"

Thomas insisted, pointing over the sea.

Joshua smiled sadly at him, "I know how you feel," he agreed.

Thomas turned to Drew. "Finally, we'll fight together?" he asked.

Drew grabbed Thomas' shoulders and dragged him into a tight embrace. "I would be honoured," he replied.

Together they turned to survey the battlefield. Joshua stood beside them, taking it in with a pained expression.

"It is almost done, but it's not done yet," he murmured. Raising his sword, he called out one last time, "For the King and his Kingdom!"

This time when the bird opened its cavernous mouth, dark liquid flowed from its throat. The foul stench of it wound through the land. It spread quickly, consuming what it touched.

Had those who witnessed the scene been asked to describe it, they couldn't have found the words. It was like nothing they could have imagined. Anyone left in the Land of Nachash who was not already on the beach, either screamed to the King for help, and were transported to the edge of the sea, or they screamed profanities against the King until the liquid contorted their bodies into lifeless pools of darkness.

"It's time for you to join the people on the seashore,"

Joshua ordered Seth, Drew, Marc, and Thomas. "There is only one battle left to fight, and I must fight it alone."

Marc swung his arm wide, encompassing the desolate carnage that surrounded them. "Joshua, who is left to fight? All your enemies have been destroyed in the slaughter!"

Seth answered as thundering hooves sounded in the distance. "Nachash! He hasn't been defeated." Turning to Joshua, Seth implored, "Let us fight for you. You're the Prince. The people need you to help them across the sea. Let us fight in your place and if we perish, we perish."

Drew, Marc, and Thomas echoed their agreement but Joshua shook his head without even considering the offer. "The fight with the Duke has been mine since before you awoke. I will fight, and I will win." Mounting his horse, Joshua turned to face the approaching darkness.

The warriors watched as Nachash raced towards Joshua. There was something distorted about his silhouette. They squinted through the swirling dust as the Duke pulled his horse to an abrupt stop. When the cloud of dust settled, they gasped at what they saw.

To their horror, a bound and gagged Abigail slumped against the Duke. They saw her eyes move across each of their faces before coming to rest on Joshua.

Nachash threw back his head in a sickening laugh.

"Pretty little Abigail has changed her mind once again, and now instead of riding out of the garden on the back of my horse, she wants to ride out of my land on the back of Joshua's. It seems I no longer please her as I once did!"

"Abigail has chosen me, Nachash, and I will bring her safely to the Kingdom just like I promised I would," answered Joshua. His eyes never left the Duke's. "You can't have anyone who doesn't choose you. That is the way it has always been, and that's what makes you so angry. Ultimately, you only have whatever power you're allowed to have."

Nachash roared like a beast and lunged across his horse's back towards Joshua. The bird dove between them and Nachash lurched back. "Shut-up!" he shrieked at Joshua. "I loathe you, I loathe that bird, and I despise your king. I will be king! I will reign!" The vein in the Duke's neck began to throb, and his eyeballs bulged. He shouted a challenge at Joshua. "If you want her, come and get her. But I will show you no mercy."

Joshua spoke firmly to Abigail, "I promised you we'd make it safely across. You can trust me." He nudged his horse closer to the Duke and unsheathed his sword. Nachash pulled out his sword and swung it wildly at Joshua. Each time Joshua attempted to return a strike, the Duke cruelly shoved Abigail in front of him, using her as a shield.

Suddenly, Joshua leapt from his horse and threw

himself at the Duke. Nachash pulled his horse back to stay out of Joshua's reach, but, caught by surprise, he lost his grip on Abigail. Thrown by the abrupt change in momentum, Abigail fell from the horse's back.

Joshua grabbed hold of Abigail and nearly threw her onto the back of his horse.

Knowing time was in short supply, Joshua shouted orders at Abigail, who nodded, wide-eyed in terror. "Don't let go of the horse's mane. You hang on no matter what! My horse will take you to the warriors by the sea!" Joshua slapped his horse's flank, sending it sprinting towards the shore.

Nachash bellowed in fury as he saw Abigail ride away. He turned on Joshua and attacked him with all his strength. The Duke's sword sliced through Joshua, opening up a wide gash across his back and shoulders. Blood gushed from open wounds and pain carved deep lines across Joshua's face. The Duke swung hard and knocked Joshua's sword to the ground.

Joshua faced the Duke alone and without his sword. His blood ran freely, staining the ground around his feet. Nachash laughed at the pitiful sight. Seeing he had the upper hand, Nachash relented in his intensity, if not his hatred. He led his horse in lazy circles around Joshua, stabbing viciously while he mocked him. Joshua fell to his knees.

Drooling at the sure taste of victory, Nachash jumped from the back of his horse and plunged his sword deep into Joshua's chest. In agony, Joshua fell over onto his side as his life seeped out through open wounds.

Nachash let out a loud victory cry before bending over to spit in Joshua's face.

But as he did, Joshua, in a final burst of strength, rose and pulled out the short blade he'd kept hidden in his belt. He plunged it deep into the Duke's chest before slumping back to the ground, twisting the dagger as he fell.

Nachash felt the fire of Joshua's blade penetrate deep. He looked down at the gaping wound that seared across his chest. The Duke watched his blood pour out and felt his strength ebb. In an awful moment of clarity, Nachash realized that this was a wound from which he would not recover.

Using every measure of strength he could muster, Nachash crawled as far away from the object of his hatred as he could. When he could move no more, he used his final breath to spew curses against the King.

The warriors watched in silent horror at the edge of the sea. The second the Duke fell silent, they started running towards their Prince. Abigail ran close behind them. Passing by the Duke's body, they recoiled at the stench that already rose from his corpse. To their horror, insects crawled from his open mouth, his ears, nose, and eyes. Death revealed who the

Duke truly was, and it was a picture most foul.

Abigail raced ahead of the warriors, desperate to get to Joshua. She threw herself down beside him. He turned to smile weakly at her as he lay bleeding. The warriors quickly caught up to her and dropped down beside them.

Joshua struggled to speak. "It is finished," he whispered. "The Duke has been defeated and the plan is complete."

Marc opened his mouth in protest but was silenced with a look from Seth.

"It's so very beautiful," spoke Joshua. "You'll see."

Abigail buried her face in his chest and wept. The moment it stopped moving a terrible keening rose from inside of her. Joshua had breathed his last. It was over.

The men wept beside her as their Prince lay motionless on the ground. This was not how it was supposed to end. They were supposed to return to the Kingdom victorious.

Theodore slowly walked from the edge of the sea towards them, pulled closer by the power of their grief. The people followed, in part out of respect, but also because they felt lost. Who were they to follow now?

After standing silent for a moment, Theodore pulled out a scroll and slowly opened it. His hands shook as he searched for a place to read from.

Finding it, Theodore spoke brokenly before reading from the scroll. "In the last days before we left the Kingdom, there was much I did not understand. The King bid me write anyway." Pausing to gather his strength, Theodore lifted the scroll higher and started to read. "You will choose death. I will pay the price. Thus will you return to Me."

"He took our death for himself," murmured Seth in awe. "We chose death, not him. Yet he is the one lying here dead."

"Now that we have known him, is it possible to return to the Kingdom to live happily without him?" questioned Abigail, fighting the despair that threated to overwhelm her.

The eagle soared above the crowd of people, crying out mournfully. It hovered above Joshua's motionless chest with outstretched wings, calling out loudly. Finally, it ceased its cry and flew away. The sun disappeared and the land surrendered itself to dark and cold.

Abigail shivered in quiet darkness. "Was there ever so great a void?" she wondered aloud. Abigail felt panic overtake her as a deep darkness, a complete absence of light, smothered them. Desperate to find an anchor in the consuming blackness, Abigail reached out, trying to grab hold of something solid and familiar. Her hands landed on a rough shirt sleeve and she grabbed tightly.

"Seth? Drew? Marc?" she cried. The men murmured her

name to let her know that they were near. Abigail let herself slide into despair that drowned her with relentless waves.

Part Three: All Things New

CHAPTER 34

They sat in darkness, huddled around Joshua's body. Together, but so very alone.

Suddenly, Abigail raised her head. "What's that noise?" she demanded. She turned in the direction the sound was coming from. She couldn't identify the sound, yet, somehow, it was familiar and safe. Abigail began to crawl towards it. It grew louder.

Abigail knew she needed to hear the sound more clearly. She rose to her feet and stumbled through the utter darkness, trying to get closer to it. She felt a hand grab her arm tightly and knew someone was walking beside her.

"I hear it, too!" exclaimed Marc's voice.

The sound seemed to be coming from a great distance, but it was as clear as crystal. Abigail could hear other people moving around in the blackness, also following the sound. It grew in volume and intensity.

"It's music," Abigail breathed. "Music is returning to the land!" She strained to hear the different notes, shuddering with joy at the harmony their blending produced. Never had she heard such music before. Abigail tried to absorb the fullness of the sound as she realized that there existed a kind of silence that has less to do with the absence of noise and more to do with the absence of beauty. The music they were now hearing was bridging a long gap of silence.

As it swirled around her, Abigail remembered the long-ago music that had existed in the garden, but had been lost in the Land of Nachash. It had been alive.

Abigail heard the melody and the harmony. She could hear the truest and best music which is made by blending them together. Consumed with a need to join in, Abigail began to sing.

At first it was only her voice that moved with the notes spinning around them, but then Abigail heard a low resonance from behind her. Slowly, tentatively at first, some of the people began to explore range and scale. Their efforts grew into a beautiful song.

"This is the Song of the Garden!" Seth exclaimed.

At this, all the people joined in. Though they were in thick darkness, they stood with eyes closed and heads raised, in defiance of it. They sang to banish it. Softly, almost imperceptibly, the coldness began to recede. Warm breath brushed across upturned faces.

Drew's eyes flew open. "Look!" he shouted above the music. "Something is coming up from the water!"

Abigail's opened her eyes. Light was advancing across the land, gently pushing back the shadows, but she couldn't see where it was coming from. It was as if the light, though growing in strength, had no specific source, but simply existed.

She focused on the sea where Drew pointed. A powerful white horse rose from the waters. Its mane and tail rippled in iridescent, shimmering waves as it ran up out of the sea. The sand seemed to dance under its hooves as it galloped across the beach.

In the soft light that had now enveloped the land, Abigail could see Seth and Drew nearby. Taking Marc's hand, they walked closer to Seth and Drew, watching the magnificent creature run past them towards the battlefield. They started to follow, wanting to see where it was headed.

Suddenly, a bright light enveloped the horse. Desperate to see, they squinted their eyes, rushing them to adjust to the unexpected brightness. The horse had run to the source of light. The light was emanating from a figure that stood beside the horse.

In that moment Abigail knew that, had someone asked her to define terms such as strength, or power, or beauty, or perfection, she would not resort to mere words. She would simply point to the man who stood there. The one who was the light.

He walked toward them. Abigail had always assumed the ground was inanimate. Not alive, so incapable of responding. She had been wrong. Each blade of grass, each speck of dust, strained towards this man's approaching footstep. They danced in celebration as he drew near and pushed up his feet in bursts of joy. Abigail couldn't decide if this figure was walking toward them or being carried along. Her body tremored in excitement as he came closer. Close enough to see the waves of dark hair. Close enough to see the softness in the eyes.

Abigail gasped. It was Joshua! Though she had come to love him, she had always thought him diminutive, unimpressive. Now he stood taller than all of them. Once they had been surprised by the strength of his grip. Now the breadth of his shoulders proclaimed it. Once his sword had flashed silver on the battlefield. Now it flickered like flames of fire.

"Joshua!" Abigail cried. Running towards him she fell at his feet. "You're alive!" she gasped in wonder.

Joshua opened his mouth to speak and the sound made Abigail cover her ears; it was too beautiful. It was powerful like rushing water, melodic like music, as bright as light.

"Abigail," he answered. He pulled her to her feet and into his embrace. She clung to him.

"There are others I must see," he whispered. She could hear the smile in his voice.

Abigail watched Joshua move among the people. Wherever his feet walked, scorched earth turned green. Whatever the wind of his presence passed over, decimation and death unfurled into new life. Trees that lay broken on the ground stood up. The whisper of a single cricket became the song of a multitude. A small bird who dared perch bravely on a broken branch to sing alone was joined by a feathered choir.

"The song of creation is being sung again!" whispered Abigail. "All is being made new!"

CHAPTER 35

As the Prince walked among his people, they saw the terrible wounds left by the Duke. Joshua was fully healed, but scars still cut deep grooves across his body. He let the people trace their path. He let them wash him with their tears.

Joshua spoke to all the people who were spread across the beach. He then led his horse to firmer ground and effortlessly jumped on its back.

The people let out a jubilant cheer at the sight of their mighty and powerful Prince.

Joshua cantered to the top of the same rock outcropping from which he had instructed them before the battle. He raised his hand to silence them. His face tone was kind but his tone was serious as he spoke.

"Do you now see and understand the price of your choices? The Duke is defeated. The land destroyed. This is what the King sought to save you from. He has longed for you every moment since that long-ago day when the gates closed behind you. The King is eagerly waiting for you to cross this sea and return to his Kingdom. The time has come to go home!"

The people roared in unison, "To the King and his Kingdom!"

To loud shouts and cheers, Joshua's horse leapt off the rock and pranced majestically towards the sand and the sea.

Seth, Drew, and Marc led the surge of people who followed the Prince. Abigail sat behind Joshua who smiled down when Seth, Drew, and Marc caught up to them. Joshua and Abigail got down from the horse and walked together with the warriors through the sand until they came to the edge of the waters.

Abigail and the warriors were unaware at first, that, though they still marched, Joshua had stopped. They turned back to see him grinning at them.

"Do you plan to cross the sea by walking on top of the water?"

The four of them exchanged sheepish glances before Seth responded. "With you, it seems possible, yes."

Joshua threw back his head and laughed. His horse reared up magnificently, before Joshua leapt onto its back. Trotting to the front of the group, he spoke. "You are fierce, loyal, and brave warriors," he said, looking each of them in the eye. "I am pleased that you are warriors of the Kingdom!"

With that, Joshua raised his fiery sword and released a long and low whistle.

At first the people heard nothing. Saw nothing. Felt nothing. Then a distant pulsing grew louder. A warm gust of wind grew stronger. A fine spray covered their faces. Suddenly, the great bird burst through the wall of clouds on the opposite shore. It beat a steady rhythm over the waters, swooping low and singing to them. Its wings stirred up the sea into a silvery mist before it soared high again to hover over Joshua.

"Take us home!" Joshua called out to the bird.

The bird dove from its great height to glide over top of the waters. As the eagle passed over the sea, the same waters that had stood as a barrier between the people and the Kingdom leapt apart under the bird's mighty wings. They gurgled and gushed on opposite sides of a dry path that opened up through the middle of the sea.

The people walked slowly across the sand, craning

their necks, attempting to take in the wonder that surrounded them.

They swung their heads between the walls of crystal-clear waters on either side of them and the silvery whiteness of the sand below their feet. With obvious joy, the bird continued to work wonders as it flew. Having soared over the waters to open a path, the bird now swept in circles across the sky, leaving a trail of colour behind it. The path across the sea was covered with a canopy of dazzling colour, a rainbow that stretched across the opened waters, bridging the land behind them with the banks of the Kingdom.

Abigail and the warriors walked along the way with their mouths hanging open. They paused to drink in all their eyes could see before being propelled forward by the crowd of people that surrounded them.

"I could not have imagined such a way of return," breathed Seth.

"I think I could stay in this exact place forever, and never lose the wonder of this moment!" exclaimed Drew, as he paused along the path.

"And yet, don't you want to keep going to see what is up ahead?" urged Marc.

Abigail wiped the tears of joy that snuck out of her eyes. Though the battle was only short hours behind them, the sting of its memory had vanished. The grey silence of the land, the cruel evil of the Duke, the bleak hopelessness of their existence was still a memory but it carried no pain. It seemed the hurt and scars of the past only carved deeper channels through which now joy and anticipation could run.

"Today, this day, we see the King!" Seth spoke with awe.

Drew turned away from the sights that surrounded them for a quick glance in Seth's direction. "Are you a little bit frightened?" he questioned.

Seth nodded thoughtfully. "Yes. But when the fear threatens to rise up and overwhelm my joy, I remember what Joshua is like. He doesn't make me feel fear. He fills me with reminders of the King's love, and how the King waits for our return. He's told us that as the son, he is like his Father. So I don't think we need to be afraid of the King."

Marc grinned at his friends. "We're leaving behind a huge adventure. Anyone care to guess what awaits us? If the Land of Nachash was shadow and the Kingdom is light, our adventures there will be far greater than anything we've experienced so far."

They walked a distance in silence, each lost in their own thoughts and wonderings. Theodore made his way through the people and came to walk alongside them. For a man who never seemed to run out of things to say, Theodore was surprisingly silent. For long moments he could not find words to express what he was experiencing.

Finally, Theodore broke his prolonged measure of pondering with a gasp. He stumbled in his excitement and grabbed onto Marc's arm to steady himself. "Look!" Theodore pointed, gesturing towards the walls of water beside them. Seth, Drew, and Marc turned their heads to where he pointed.

The sea that had previously blocked their return to the Kingdom had been murky and mysterious. But the waters that bordered their journey home shimmered like clearest glass. Their beautiful transparency exposed churning schools of fish that moved towards the Kingdom alongside the people. The waters whirled with creatures that swam, dove, cavorted, and danced in a visual symphony of excitement, as if they, too, longed for the King.

Marc stood silently taking it in. Tears made their way down his cheeks in silent rivers before he began to weep audibly. His friends moved closer, surprised by this sudden display of emotion.

Marc dropped slowly to his knees on the sand and cradled his head in his hands as he cried. Seth, Drew, and Theodore knelt beside him, quietly respectful, even though they did not understand what moved him so.

A hush fell over the people, who had stopped walking to stand quietly on the path. Aware of the change among the people, Joshua turned from his place at the front, and faced them.

"Why do you stop when the Kingdom awaits?" he questioned kindly.

Marc struggled to choke back sobs before he could respond.

"To see this," he confessed, pointing to the aquatic display. "It makes me realize what we walked away from when we left the garden. I see now *who* we walked away from. I can more clearly remember the King for who he was, and we deserted him! We chose the Duke, the vile, evil, deceptive Duke, over our perfect King. We willingly picked empty lies and self-indulgence, and it was never worth it! Not even for a second!"

Marc wiped his tears away and stood to his feet. "What do we expect?" he cried out. "To return and have everything restored to the way it was? Even though that is now the deepest longing of my heart, I can't give a single reason for the King to accept me back after what I've done. There is not one thing that I could offer him! Even if I could say I'd return and pledge to him my undying loyalty and service, he doesn't need it!"

As Marc finished his confession, the people began to weep along with him. "We were wrong," they said. "We believed a lie and lost the only thing worth having."

Theodore stood humbly before the Prince. "Joshua,

Prince of the Kingdom, son of the King, may we return as his servants?"

Joshua gazed upon the people that he loved, his heart deeply moved by the change in theirs. They had left the Kingdom in prideful, selfish pursuit. They had not really understood who the King was and what they were leaving behind. They now stood, on the brink of return, truly repentant. They were ready to enter the Kingdom.

Joshua answered Theodore gently, "You will return, but it will not be as his servants." He called out for the people to rise up. "Look, my people! Your King approaches!"

The people looked up through their tears. Just beyond the walls of water, where the sea ended and the Kingdom shore began, the clouds lifted to revealed their King. They knew him upon sight. He ran towards them with outstretched arms.

A King—running!

CHAPTER 36

A song that had never been sung before sprang to the people's lips, released with joy and abandon in the presence of their King.

As the King ran through the open gates of the Kingdom towards them, the water retreated behind them. It raced back, washing over the Land of Nachash in a final cleansing before gathering in a deep, lush valley. There was no longer a distinction between the Kingdom and the Land of Nachash, all was under the reign of the King. All land was now Kingdom land.

Abigail stood in reverent awe as the King

approached. As he ran towards them, his feet seemed to kick up the clouds which disappeared behind him. The splendor of the entire Kingdom was revealed.

Abigail remembered how she had once gazed upon the King's palace from a distance. She remembered how it had shone through the clouds. Now it stood in full sight, majestic at the top of the mountain in the centre of the Kingdom, proclaiming the majesty of its King.

The palace soared to a height she never imaged a dwelling could reach. It sprawled across the hills, following the dips and peaks of the land. Abigail tried to take in the number of people around her. There were many of them, yet still, looking at the palace, she knew there would be more than enough room for them all.

Abigail remembered the jewels she had worn for the Duke in his castle, and how she had thought them beautiful and rich. The castle before her was constructed from jewels that were so clear and bright, the ones she'd once worn around her neck would have seemed like common rocks by comparison.

The lush gardens of the Kingdom surrounded the palace with vegetation which Abigail had forgotten existed after her long exile in the Land of Nachash. Truly, she thought, she could spend forever exploring the Kingdom that lay before her and never get tired of it, nor ever get to the end of it.

Hearing a keening cry of joy close by, Abigail turned to her right. It was Seth. Unable to contain himself, he started running towards the King, faster than his legs had ever carried him. Seth raced across the last stretch of sand and reached a thick carpet of grass on the Kingdom shore. Closing the distance between himself and the King, Seth intended to fall at the King's feet, but before his knees could hit the ground, he felt himself being swept up into the embrace of the King. A mysterious combination of strength and gentleness enveloped Seth as the King spoke for his ears alone.

"My son! You have returned! Oh, how I have longed for this day! Welcome home, Seth."

Abigail watched Drew follow close behind his friend, Seth. She saw the King put Seth back on the ground and run to meet Drew. She smiled as Drew, who preferred to remain composed and keep his emotions at bay, bolted towards the King, throwing himself into the King's arms like a child. The strength he'd always worn like a suit of armor melted in the embrace of the King. Though experience had matured him, in the King's arms, Drew's demeanor became as carefree as a young boy.

"You have returned, my son!" The King spoke for Drew alone. "Each day I waited for you to come back to my Kingdom. Welcome home, Drew."

Abigail turned her gaze to Marc, impulsive Marc, who had never been able to wait. And yet, there he stood. Fidgeting, but trying to wait for his turn. She saw the moment Marc knew the King was coming for him and couldn't help but grin as she watched him attempt to squelch any rash actions. Abigail laughed as Marc's flood of excitement burst forth. He could not deny who he'd been made to be.

Marc threw caution to the wind and jumped into the King's open arms. The King laughed with delight and swung Marc around. "You are finally home!" chuckled the King. "I'm glad you're back! Welcome home, Marc!"

Abigail's eyes misted as she saw Theodore moving in the corner of her vision. He walked slowly at first. But with each step that carried him closer to the King, he threw off a little bit more of the constraints of age that had bound him. His final steps were confident strides. The King reached out for Theodore, pulled him into a hug, then held him back to look into his eyes. "Theodore," smiled the King, "you have returned. The journey was long and the way was hard, but you are home. Welcome back, Theodore!"

Abigail watched as each person was greeted individually by the King. He had something special and unique for all of them. Every person was showered with welcome and love that was personal.

She saw all this, yet, she couldn't quell the worry that

rose within her. Joshua walked over to her and stood beside her. He took her hand and gave it a reassuring squeeze. She glanced at him quickly, revealing her inner disquiet. She remembered how she had once sung for the King in carefree abandon. But she'd also sung for Nachash. Now that she saw the King, she wondered how she'd be able to look into his eyes, knowing that he knew all this, too.

Joshua leaned down to whisper to her, "Abigail, I am here with you and am not going anywhere. Trust in my love and the love of the King. Do you remember how I promised it would all be worth it in the end?"

Abigail nodded, but couldn't speak past the lump in her throat. The King approached.

She dropped her gaze and took a small step back, as if by hiding behind Joshua she might not be noticed. Joshua took a step forward, and Abigail looked up to watch the reunion of the King and the Prince.

She saw the King clasp Joshua's shoulders and heard him speak through tears. "You have done it, my son. You have returned my people to me and to the Kingdom." The love shared between the King and the Prince was its own melody.

Abigail watched them and listened to the music their love made. This was her King! The King that knew each of his people by name. The King that had made each of them in love.

She peeked up at his face and studied it. She

remembered those eyes, that smile, and his voice. In a distant place and time, they had been her greatest joy and most secure place of love. She remembered how singing for him in the garden was never about her, but always about him.

And that memory set her free! The King would not accept her because of who she was or was not. He would not welcome her based on great deeds she had accomplished any more than he would banish her for destructive choices she had made. Her King accepted her because of who he was. He welcomed her because she had returned on the path which he had opened for her.

As if he could read her mind, the King turned to Abigail. Her body moved towards him as though it was no longer under her control.

"My King!" she sobbed.

The King gathered her into his loving embrace and gently wiped her tears as she cried. As long as she had tears to cry, he held her tight and wiped away every one.

As the last tear was absorbed by his gentle hand, Abigail tremulously met the King's gaze.

"My daughter," he spoke, "you are truly home. I have waited for you to return and have reserved a room for you in the palace."

Abigail spoke through a fresh supply of tears. "My King, once I sang for you alone, but after I left the Kingdom,

I sang for. . ." Abigail couldn't bear to say his name in the presence of the King.

The King tenderly interrupted her. "I know, my child," he replied. "I watched you sing for him with a breaking heart. But you chose to return. Will you sing for me once again?" asked the King.

Abigail looked into the eyes of her King and saw the love she'd dreamed of but had never felt since leaving the garden. And in the fullness of that love she finally knew complete forgiveness. The King knew the worst about her, and yet he loved her. The King didn't need her, and yet he waited for her to come home. The King was whole without her, and yet he found joy in who he'd made her to be.

"Yes," answered Abigail. "I will sing for you, my King. I will sing forever and for always, just for you."

CHAPTER 37

Having greeted all the people, the King threw open the palace doors. His delight knew no bounds as he showed the people through their new home. There were rooms for them all. Rooms that matched exactly who he had created them to be.

Some rooms were filled with books and cozy chairs. Others were filled with empty pages and coloured pencils. Some rooms had piles of wooden blocks and sturdy nails. Still others contained flower gardens or refreshing pools. No two rooms were the same.

Some people explored the palace and others ran

through the garden. They retraced pathways that, though forgotten for a time, were instantly familiar. Some of the people returned to what had once been known as the Land of Nachash. It was Kingdom land now, and they were filled with wonder at how lush and abundant it had become. They could remember bits and pieces of the land and their life within it, but the ache was gone.

Time in the Land of Nachash had possessed a relentless quality to it. Time in the Kingdom did not exist in that way. The people did not grab at it, long for it, or try to hold on to it. They simply lived fully in each moment as it came.

Though there were many people, the King took each one aside individually to show them what he had prepared for them while they'd been in exile. It was a funny thing in that, while each of the people waited for their turn, nobody felt they'd waited too long.

****

The King walked Seth to the waters of the sea which were now nestled in a fragrant valley. Animals grazed around its shore. Creatures leapt from its depths.

"Seth, all these creatures need names. I need somebody to study their characteristics and pick just the right name for each one of them. I would like you to be that person."

Seth nearly jumped in delight. "Oh, King," he shouted in elation. "This would be my greatest joy!" He turned to the King, radiant. "This is a large undertaking. It will take a lot of time."

The King threw back his head and laughed. "Time you have, my son, time you have."

Seth embraced the King. "All my life's work will now be for you," he whispered.

****

Drew followed the King in anticipation. Where was the King taking him? They reached the edge of a great field and entered a building sprawled along its edge. Drew looked around in astonishment. The walls were hung with curious devices. His eyes caught on balls, baskets, boxes, sticks, and many more things he could only catch glimpses of in his excitement.

"What is all of this?" he asked, turning to the King.

"Well, son, you were made to love competition. All of these materials can be used in the creation of games to be played by the people. I need someone to create those games and organize competitions for the people. I would like you to be that person."

Drew pumped his fist excitedly. "I can't wait!" he grinned at the King. "How did you know how much I loved this kind of thing?"

The King beamed at Drew and pulled him into a hug. "Because I made you, my child."

****

Marc hung onto the King's robes as the King led him blindfolded through the garden. "Are we almost there?" he questioned impatiently.

"Just a little further," murmured the King. "Watch your step!"

Marc's body hummed with anticipation as the King peeled back the blindfold. His eyes adjusted to the presence of light and he gasped in amazement. The King had led him into a large stable filled with creatures of every species imaginable. Some of them appeared to be able to walk, others would run, still others could fly. And then there were those that Marc thought might be able to do all three.

"Wh - what is this?" he stammered in excitement.

"Marc, you crave speed. You delight in racing. That's what these creatures were made for. They love speed just like you. I need somebody to train them and ready them for races. I would like you to be that person."

Marc jumped on the back of a bizarre animal that balanced on three spindly legs but also came with two sets of wings. He clutched its long, hairy neck as the creature hopped erratically out of the stables. They bounced outside and the creature began to beat its wings and lift off, into the air.

"Thank you, my King," Marc shouted as he flew out of sight.

CHAPTER 38

A small bird chirped and fluttered above Abigail's head as she arranged her curls in a tiara.

"It's almost time for the performance, Abigail," a voice called up the stairs. Abigail smiled into the mirror then bounded down the palace staircase, curls and ribbons flying behind her. Her King and the Prince awaited, and tonight's performance had been a long time in the making.

All the people had gathered in the great throne room for the concert, which would be magnificent. Soaring windows were thrown open to allow creation to be the backdrop. Waters outside the palace windows gurgled and gushed the melody. Swaying flowers kept the rhythm. Kingdom animals moved in breathtaking choreography.

But all eyes were on the King. He sat with Joshua on one side and Theodore on the other. Seth, Drew, and Marc stood behind the throne. The people gathered in groups in the palace chamber, the same room where the Duke had staged his treasonous rebellion a lifetime ago.

The King looked at Abigail, his eyes encouraging her to begin. Abigail opened her mouth and released the melody which sprang from within her. There was no hint of insecurity. This performance wasn't about her, it was about the King. Abigail danced as she sang.

When the strains of music faded away, Abigail opened her eyes to gaze upon the King. He smiled at her and she bowed for him.

Joshua put his hands together to start the applause and she curtsied happily for him. Abigail looked up at her friends, Seth, Drew, and Marc, and gave them each a quick wave.

Abigail then turned to face the people and let her eyes travel across their faces.

She was living in the middle of happily ever after.

****

Michael watched the events of the throne room in awe. In the darkest moments of greatest pain, he could never have imagined beauty this bright.

He had wanted to resist when the King allowed the people to leave the garden created just for them. He'd wanted to descend upon the Duke with all of the palace guard when Joshua had battled him. And when darkness covered the land and Joshua lay cold on the dirt, Michael thought his heart would break.

Now he watched the people who had returned—the ones who had freely chosen to serve their King. He saw them gaze upon the King and the Prince in love and adoration. He heard their songs of joy. Being in the presence of the King and his subjects, Michael knew that all was complete and made whole.

This had been the plan all along.

It took his breath away!

"Then I saw a new heaven and a new earth, for the first heaven and the first earth had passed away, and the sea was no more. And I saw the holy city, new Jerusalem, coming down out of heaven from God, prepared as a bride adorned for her husband.
And I heard a loud voice from the throne saying, "Now the dwelling of God is with men, and he will live with them. They will be his people, and God himself will be with them and be their God. He will wipe every tear from their eyes. There will be no more death or mourning or crying or pain, for the old order of things has passed away."
And he who was seated on the throne said, "Behold, I am making all things new."
Revelation 21:1-5

ABOUT THE AUTHOR

Arlene has enjoyed being married to her high school sweetheart for more than twenty years, and is the proud mother to four children. She fulfills many different roles: daughter, sister, wife, mother, teacher, Bible study leader. All these roles have grown and shaped her. But the role Arlene most desires to define her, is child of the one true King.

From Him, through Him, and to Him are all things – to God be the Glory!

Arlene's Bible study and devotional materials are available at www.unshakenministries.com. You can also follow her blog at www.aspaceforgrace.ca

Made in the USA
Lexington, KY
06 May 2018